A SUPERIOR CRIME AND OTHER STORIES

VIRGINIA WINTERS

FROM THE RIVER PUBLISHING

PUBLISHER

From The River Publishing
26 William Booth Crst,
Lindsay, On.
Canada
K9V 6E1
705-324-3857
vwinters@bell.net
ISBN: 978-1-7751776-2-3

.

COPYRIGHT

For my brother

A SUPERIOR CRIME

Anne McPhail, paediatrician, traveller, amateur genealogist and, unexpectedly, a solver of mysteries, first appeared in print in this adventure which takes her on a journey to Northern Ontario.

A Superior Crime was first published on Pine Tree Mysteries, issue 5, 2009 and later on Wattpad.

This is a work of fiction and characters shouldn't be taken to represent any of the individuals who work for VIA or the OPP.

A SUPERIOR CRIME

*A*nne stowed her coat in the overhead bin and sank gratefully into the worn plush of her seat. A broken-down car at one end of the road and an appointment at the other meant, gloriously, a train journey. She loved train travel, even the modern version; loved the glimpses of country life; loved the lights on the remote farmhouses in the darkness.

The train, the Lake Superior, travelled between Sudbury and White River three times per week. Comfort class. Only one car for passengers, the rest freight and baggage. The windows were wide and the seat spacious, so Anne was happy.

None of the four other passengers sat together. Going to be a long quiet ride, she thought as she pulled her laptop from its leather bag. She was going to meet a man in White River who promised to show her papers on the De la Ronde family, ancestors on her father's side. She worked at her family database for a few hours.

The conductor stopped to tell her lunch was ready in a few minutes: smoked turkey breast on a croissant, salad, and pudding. A table separated the four chairs where she was sitting.

Anne called out, "Would anyone like to join me for lunch?"

Two men and a woman staggered down the car to her seat. The fourth man hesitated, and then sat across the aisle from them.

"Dave Barker," the man said.

"Anne McPhail," she said, smiling up into the lined face of the elderly latecomer.

Giselle Cloutier, a dark-haired, dark-eyed woman of about forty-five perched on the edge of her seat, clutching an artist's carrying bag.

Harrison McDonald, a redhead with an engaging grin, pumped Anne's hand and told her what a great idea this was to eat together.

The last man of the foursome settled back into a seat across from Anne. He gave his name as Parsons and his immediate attention to the view out the window. A thin, almost wasted man, he looked as if a good meal was a rare event in his life.

"You on your way to White River, Anne?" McDonald asked as he peered at the screen of her laptop.

"Yes," she said and closed the cover.

"You had family names on the screen, there. You one of those people who goes round looking at tombstones and such?"

Curiosity defines this guy, Anne thought as she answered with a laugh. "Yes, I am, but not in White River in winter.

"Is that what you do for a living?"

"No, I'm a doctor, but I retired recently. Genealogy is my hobby."

"Kinda waste of time, ain't it?" said the man across the aisle.

"Depends on your point of view. Mr Barker, is it? I'm retired and have always been interested in history, my own included. I've travelled a lot and met many interesting people doing this."

"Hey, each to his own." The man put up his hands in a back-off gesture, to Anne's irritated tone, not her words. "No offence, lady."

"Sorry, Mr Barker. I get that "waste of time" comment a lot."

The train slowed and then stopped. No station in sight, just two men standing at the trackside.

"What's going on?" Anne asked.

"Didn't they tell you?" Parsons turned his head back towards her. "This train will stop anywhere along the track to pick you up so long as you arrange it ahead."

"You mean the people on the train now, aren't the only ones who will be on it?" No one could miss the fear in Giselle's voice.

"That's right. Usually hunters or canoeists. There's a car for canoes. Load your own."

As he spoke the car door opened and a bearded man, dressed in the padded work-shirt and pants and orange vest of a hunter, ambled down the aisle and sat in the row behind Anne.

The attendant started serving lunches as the train picked up speed. McDonald had another question for Anne. "What family are you researching?"

"De La Ronde."

"Haven't heard that one before, up here."

"Mostly Laronde or Larone now. You remember that Mountie murdered in Saskatchewan. Was it last year? He was a De La Ronde. Up this way, mostly Metis people."

"You don't look Metis," Giselle said.

"I'm a long way from the original Laronde," Anne said.

"How do you do this stuff, anyway?"

"You start by asking every relative you can about what they know or remember. Once you have some family names and dates, then you search for birth certificates, land records, census reports. Lots of information on the Internet. Sometimes just your surname helps. Giselle's is French-Canadian. The records in Quebec are superb. She could trace them fairly easily."

"I'm from North Bay," Giselle said.

"Harder."

Lunch intervened, and they ate in a companionable silence. One after another the passengers walked to the washroom at the other end of the car. Giselle scurried down the aisle, peering back at them before she disappeared through the narrow door.

Anne had discovered that her wireless connected her to the Internet, even here in the North.

"How about McDonald?" Harrison took up the topic again. "Could you research my family?"

"Much more difficult," Anne told him. "I have McDonalds too, but many came at the time of the Highland Clearances. You need a starting point. Even where your father was from would help."

"Sounds like work?"

"Sure. But as I said, researching gives a purpose to travel, and I have met many interesting people."

Murderers too, she thought, as she recalled two visits to a small town in Vermont. Her genealogical knowledge had helped in tracking down the killers of bodies she had found.

"Is there information about Irish people?" Parsons asked.

"Yes, quite a bit, although a huge fire in Dublin destroyed most of the census records."

Anne could see by the familiar glaze in her listeners' eyes that that was enough genealogy. She closed her laptop, put her seat back a little and closed her eyes.

She had just drifted off to sleep, or so it seemed when someone called her name.

"Dr McPhail. Could you help me?" the conductor said.

"What's wrong?"

"The other lady seems to have been in the lavatory a very long time. Could you come and see? She doesn't answer."

"Certainly."

The lavatory door was unlocked, according to the small tab at the handle, but blocked from the other side. The conductor pushed it open a few inches for Anne.

"She's lying on the floor with her feet against the door. If you give me a little wider opening, I think I can get in there."

The conductor pushed steadily on the door until the opening was wide enough for her to slip through. Moments were all it took for her to be sure the woman was dead. Blood congealed around a

4

wound in her chest. Stains in the sink suggested a killer who took the time to wash up. Blood on his hands or his weapon, Anne thought.

"Dr McPhail."

"Push open the door again. She's dead. Please look in so you can see her too. I don't want to move her. I think she's been murdered."

Anne had a digital camera in her purse, and she took pictures before leaving the claustrophobic space.

"How long until White River?" she asked.

"Three hours."

When Anne returned to her seat, McDonald asked what had happened.

"Giselle is dead."

Shock and disbelief played over the faces of the other passengers.

"Did she have a heart attack or something?"

"Someone attacked her heart with a knife or a gun," Anne replied. The others were all talking.

"Someone killed her?"

"What the hell?"

"We're the only ones on the train."

Only the sound of the train itself filled the car as the passengers fell silent, each looking suspiciously at the other.

"I didn't go to the washroom," Anne said. "Did everyone else?"

Everyone else had.

"So now we have a dead woman and four of us who could have killed her. Great," said Barker, smashing his fist against the seat arm.

"More than four," Anne said. "Trainmen have lives too."

The latecomer in the hunting clothes asked, "Who are you people? What do you do?"

Anne replied first, explaining that she was a retired doctor. Barker worked for the government—Natural Resources, he said.

McDonald was a real estate agent. No surprise there, Anne thought. Parsons just said he lived in the bush, did some guiding.

"And you?" Anne asked.

"I work for the city of Toronto. Name's Drucker. Just out here on vacation with my buddy."

"Where is he?"

"He lives where I got on."

The conductor had news for them. No one was to leave the train until they got to White River. The OPP would meet them there.

"But I live an hour before," protested Parsons.

"You have to stay on this time, Tom. We'll send you back, no charge."

Another one eliminated, Anne thought. Not too likely a guy who lived in the bush would be involved in murdering a random passenger on a train.

A few minutes later, Drucker left his seat.

"Where are you going?" McDonald said.

"Washroom."

McDonald's suspicious gaze followed Drucker down the aisle, watched him try the door and fail to open it.

"Looks like the conductor locked us in here," he said, and then lurched forward in his seat as the train slowed abruptly. "What the hell?"

The door at the end of the car opened and the conductor came through, spoke briefly to Drucker, and then walked expertly down the aisle to them.

"What's up, Pete?" Parsons asked.

"Moose on the line. It'll take a few minutes until he decides to move on."

The passengers turned back to their discussion of who did what.

"Where are you from, McDonald, and where do you work?" demanded Barker.

"What's it to you?" He's older than he looks, Anne thought, as

McDonald pushed his thinning red hair back from a forehead damp with sweat.

"I want to know who you people are. One of you is a killer."

"It's not me. I sell real estate in Sudbury, but I'm from White River. I'm just going up for the weekend. What about you?"

"I told you I work for Natural Resources. I'm from North Bay, but I never met this Giselle."

"All we know is what we tell each other," Anne said. "I don't even remember everyone's first name."

"Dave," Barker replied.

"And you're Tom," Anne noted, turning to Parsons.

"Yes. What did you say your name was, McDonald?"

"Harrison."

"Where's that Drucker?"

"Another one gone into the lethal lavatory," McDonald said.

"Christ," Barker said as he charged down to the washroom.

"Empty," he called back. "He must have gone through."

"Or out," Anne said.

"Did he leave anything in his seat?"

"Nope," said Parsons, as he peered over the back of his chair. "But he didn't have much with him when he came on."

"Shouldn't he have had a rifle if he was hunting?" Anne asked.

"You can't bring a rifle on the train," Parsons told her," and I didn't hear him say he'd been hunting."

"I guess I assumed it from the way he was dressed."

Anne left her seat and walked down to the other end of the car where she stood looking out the door for a moment. Someone, McDonald she thought, yelled, asking her what she was doing.

"Just looking out," she said as she turned and walked back. "I wondered where Drucker had gone." The train started abruptly, and she stumbled into her seat. "I think I'll do some work."

Anne wedged herself into her seat, so her screen wasn't visible to the others, especially the nosy McDonald, and started searching for him on-line. Lucky he had an unusual first name.

No Harrison McDonald. Not in any real estate website she could find, not in a general Google search, nor in the yellow pages, nor in 411. Anne looked up to find him staring at her.

"The window behind you is a good mirror," he said. "Didn't find me, eh?"

Fear gripped her throat, and she struggled to force the words out. "What are you talking about?"

"I saw what you were doing. So now you know." He pulled a gun from inside his jacket, gestured for Barker and Parsons to sit near Anne, and took a seat himself across the aisle.

"What do you think you are going to do now? Kill us all?" Parsons asked.

"If I have to. Behave yourselves, and no one else needs to die."

"You won't get away with this," Barker said. "The cops are waiting for you in White River."

"We're stopping before White River," McDonald said, reaching for the call button.

Moments later, the conductor appeared, stopping at the sight of the gun.

"Tell the engineer to stop the train at post 722 or one of these people will no longer be with us." The conductor backed off and then ran towards the front of the train.

"So now we have a few minutes to wait."

"Where is your buddy Drucker?" Anne asked.

"He's not my buddy. I think he had his reasons for getting off the train before White River."

"Why did you kill Giselle?"

"No more questions."

The train started to slow and then stopped at a distance marker.

"Parsons, open that case, McDonald said, pointing to Giselle's portfolio case, "There's an envelope inside it. Give it to me. All of you, off the train."

He herded them down to the end of the car. They stepped one by one down onto the roadbed into cold, glancing sleet. An ATV was parked beside the marker. This man was going to kill them, Anne thought, fear clutching at her throat again.

"The conductor will have told the police who was on the train," she whispered.

"Then I'm leaving no one to tell where I have gone," he snarled raising his handgun.

Anne covered her face. An explosion of sound hit her. Her first thought was that he hadn't killed her. Then she opened her eyes. McDonald lay in a twisted mass on the ground, blood pouring from a chest wound. Drucker loped up the line, cradling a rifle in one arm.

He turned McDonald over, felt for a pulse, and pulled the envelope from his hand.

"Let's go inside, folks," he said.

"Who the hell are you?" demanded Barker.

"Detective-Sergeant Drucker, Toronto."

The passengers turned silently and climbed back onto the train.

"Do you know who Giselle or McDonald was, Sergeant?

"No. I'll check her purse while we move on to White River."

"What about McDonald's body," Anne asked.

"Trainman is staying with it until I get back."

Barker grabbed Giselle's carryon but stopped as Drucker bellowed at him.

"I want to know who she is. Maybe there is some connection."

"I'll deal with it," said Drucker.

Drucker extracted the contents of the bag and handed them over to Anne, instructing her to write down what she was given.

The first wallet revealed identification for Marie-Ange Bertrand, Montreal. He dug deeper and handed Anne a small case. Make-up, she thought, as she opened it.

"Huh," she said. "Another complete set of id. This one's for Giselle Cloutier, including a passport."

"Let me see that," Barker said.

"Hands off, Barker," McDonald ordered.

"There is a passport for Bertrand, too, "Anne said. "Next of kin, Alysse. Oh, my."

"Do you know this Alysse?" Barker asked.

"I've met an Alysse Bertrand. She's the widow of a man murdered in Vermont last year. She owns an art Gallery in Montreal. The husband was an art thief."

"So who was this woman, Cloutier or Bertrand?" Parsons spoke up for the first time. "And what's in the leather case?"

Drucker opened the zipper. Two paintings, signed Cloutier, were all it contained.

"See if you can find this Cloutier on the Internet," Barker suggested.

Anne searched for artists, first Canadian and then world-wide, but found no Giselle and no Marie-Ange Bertrand.

"When people obtain a fake identity, sometimes they use old records. For example, a child who died young. How old was Giselle supposed to be? Where was she born?" Anne said.

"Forty-seven and in North Bay."

"So 1957, more or less."

"1956"

"How are you going to find those records?"

"I'm going to look at tombstones."

A site containing NorthEastern Ontario Grave Markers appeared on her screen. A Catholic cemetery in a small town just outside North Bay, held a solitary Cloutier, Giselle, infant daughter of Giles and Marie, born 1956, died, 1958.

"Here's a possibility," she said. "It could have been done."

"Big deal. Now we know who she was. So what? The only one who had any connection to her is you." Barker was getting angry again.

"Well, I didn't go down to that washroom," Anne retorted. "And I had no connection to her. I only met the woman who might have been her sister once. The husband was stealing paintings and exporting them to the USA. His widow had nothing to do with it as far as I know but maybe we should look at those paintings again."

The paintings were ordinary, amateurish works on new canvas. No frames. No over-painting. They were not even very good. Why was she carrying them around at all?

"What is in that envelope?" she asked Drucker.

"Sketches," he said.

"Could we see them?"

"What for? They're evidence."

"Evidence of what? McDonald is dead. You won't be able to charge him with anything. What harm can there be in showing us what was worth killing for?" Anne said.

Reluctantly Drucker opened the manila folder and brought out one small sketch. The artist had been practicing: hands, noses, feet. Where had she seen this kind of lovely work?

"Of course. Da Vinci."

"Da Vinci. You mean the guy on TV?" Barker asked.

"No, an artist, a very famous artist. I have seen sketches like these in books about him. Surely they can't be real. They would be worth a fortune."

"A fortune?" Barker repeated.

"Or they're forgeries. Or I'm out to lunch."

"Quite a motive for theft, but why did McDonald kill her?"

"We don't know that he did," Anne commented, "although it seems most likely."

"Come on, Anne. What other explanation is there?

"How did she die, Dr McPhail?" interrupted the policeman.

"All I saw was a hole in her chest."

"Burns around it?"

"No. I thought—likely a knife. Someone cleaned up. There was blood in the sink."

"Then we'll know by the blood on the hands."

"That will be me," Anne said. "I touched her."

"You didn't leave your seat until after she was dead," Parsons reminded her.

"It must have been McDonald or whatever his name was. Falling out among thieves." Anne had started to shake again. Why did this always happen to her?

"You folks try to get a little rest before White River," Drucker said. "It's going to be a long night."

Anne opened her computer again. Barker worked for Natural Resources, he said. She went to the government site, looking for names. Drucker looked over her shoulder, watching her scroll through the sites. He had grunted with satisfaction when she found Barker. So at least a Barker worked for the MNR. What about Parsons? Guides weren't likely listed on the Internet, unless at the site for the town itself. No luck there. Drucker moved back to his seat, leaving her to her search.

What happened today, she asked herself. A woman had died: a courier, a thief stealing from other thieves, a girlfriend? Who or what was she?

A man had died—a thief. Was he a killer, too? He seemed ready to kill them. Who left that ATV?

"Who rode that ATV to the milepost?" she asked aloud.

"What?" asked Drucker.

"Someone rode that ATV to the milepost. I didn't see any other tracks, and the ground was so soft with all that rain. Maybe there is someone else on board?"

"The ATV could have been there a long time," Drucker reassured her, reaching for the call button for the conductor. When he appeared, Drucker told him to lock both ends of the car and give him the keys.

"Now relax, no one is getting in here."

The north of Superior landscape slipped by Anne's window: long stretches of maple bushes, interrupted by stands of white spruce and pine with occasional accents of bright yellow tamarack. The bones showed through, too: outcroppings of granite, some many feet high, where the earth had been torn away by the receding glaciers. What had happened, she asked herself again. Two people were dead and a third man, a policeman, had a possible fortune in his hands. Three of them— Parsons, Barker, herself and the conductor and somewhere the other train staff, remain. How many... Anne drifted off to sleep with her incomplete thoughts filling her mind, to wake moments or hours later to the train slowing.

"White River," Parsons told her. "We made it."

As the train stopped at the station house, a lone policeman boarded, spoke to the conductor and Drucker, and then walked down the aisle to the little clutch of passengers.

"Staff-Sergeant Whitehead," he introduced himself. "Would you people come with me, please? I will need statements from all of you."

Anne stretched up to get her coat from the overhead bin. As she pulled it on, she said, "Staff-Sergeant, I don't know about everyone else, but I am hungry, thirsty, tired and need a bathroom before I can give you a coherent statement."

Murmurs of agreement came from the others.

"We'll have all you need at the office, Doctor."

As Anne stepped down from the train, she noticed Drucker disappearing around the front of the station. He still carried the manila envelope with the drawing.

Three hours, a plain white bread ham sandwich and several strong cups of tea later, she signed her name to her statement. She had a question. "Staff Sergeant, why haven't we seen anything of Drucker?"

"He had to get back to the city, right after he gave us his statement. He'll be back."

"Why did he take the drawing?"

"What drawing?"

"The one I told you about," she said.

"I am sure he left it in evidence. He told me that you were pretty excited about it, but it was a forgery."

"Really." Anne looked thoughtfully at the big policeman. What the hell, she thought, might as well ask him. "Are you sure he's a policeman?"

"Why?"

"Just the way he behaved at the scene. I mean, he could have called you to come there. It seemed to me that a police officer wouldn't leave a civilian with a body at a crime scene. Did he call you?"

"No, we learned about it when you arrived."

"He told us he called you."

The policeman closed his eyes briefly, his lips and jaw set, and then he left the room. Anne sat quietly, waiting. When he returned, it was to tell her that Drucker was a phoney.

"Can you describe him, Dr McPhail?"

"I can do better that that. I have a camera built into my computer. When he looked at some information, I took his picture. I took all their pictures." Anne's fingers played over the keyboard, bringing up Drucker's handsome face. "I can make you a copy if you let me plug into your printer."

Two days later, a long sleep and a successful visit to White River's museum and its local historian saw Anne back at the station, ready to return to Sudbury. A beaming Staff-Sergeant Whitehead met her on the platform.

"Dr McPhail, I wanted to thank you. We got him, in Toronto, just as he was boarding a plane for London."

"Congratulations."

"Why did you suspect him?"

"Something about him. I have some friends in Vermont who are policemen. He shot McDonald and casually left his body by the tracks; the police officers I know wouldn't have done that. And why did he have a rifle handy anyway? They don't let you carry firearms on the train. He did save our lives. I hope that will count for something. Were they all in it together? McDonald and Drucker and the woman?"

"Yes, we think so, but Drucker isn't saying much. We're very grateful to you for your help in identifying him."

"You're welcome. Was the drawing genuine?"

"Yes, it was."

"Where did it come from?"

"Stolen from a private collection last year. It was on Interpol's list. We don't know yet how these people got it. Goodbye," he said as the conductor handed her up the steps.

"Goodbye."

Anne settled back into her seat and watched the town recede into the distance and blend into the bush. Her thoughts turned to the lovely sketch she had held in her hands. A Da Vinci drawing.

MISSING ON THE MADAWASKA

Anne's second adventure takes her back to her hometown of Arnprior, Ontario, to act as a locum for a vacationing doctor.

This is a work of fiction and the characters do not represent any individuals in Arnprior or the surrounding area.

2

MISSING ON THE MADAWASKA

*N*atalie, the secretary from Roberta's office across the hall, knocked on the door frame and peered at me through her thick lenses.

"What can I do for you, Natalie?"

"Dr Thomas is gone."

"Gone?" What reason for panic was that? Good for her. Roberta, an internist, rarely got out of her office before 7:00 pm and here it was only 5:00 pm.

"She walked out on Mrs Hudson and left her there without telling her what to do or when to come back. She didn't tell me where she was going and I can't find her in the ICU or the ER or at home or on her cell or anywhere."

"You've tried all those places already?"

"Yes. But the five patients in the waiting room, what am I going to tell them?"

"Tell them Dr Thomas has been called to an emergency, ask if anyone needs a routine prescription filled and say you will deal with it all tomorrow."

My secretary, the last one before I retired, could have handled this little situation without breaking rhythm in her typing.

"Thank you, but I'm so worried about her. What will I do if she doesn't come tomorrow?"

"We'll manage."

After she went to soothe the abandoned patients, I left, still concerned about Roberta. Even if an emergency called her away, she would take a moment to tell Natalie or say goodbye to the patient. Perhaps something unusual happened with the last patient?

Roberta and I studied at medical school together at Queen's. I jumped at the chance to do a paediatric locum in Arnprior when she called me about the job. I was born in the little town at the confluence of the Madawaska and Ottawa rivers, and so this was coming home for me.

Natalie ran out to the parking lot to talk to me.

"Dr Mcphail, could you come with me to Dr.Thomas' house? I have a key so if we thought she was sick or hurt or something we could go in..."

Giving in seemed the quickest way to home and dinner, so I left with her and drove down the main street, past the handsome old post-office that now enjoyed a new life as a museum and turned left onto an avenue of old homes. Roberta's house, a smaller redbrick Victorian sat protected from the street by a broad expanse of lawn. I rang the doorbell and waited. Natalie hung back and then disappeared around the side of the house. What did she think she was doing now?

A young woman, tall, dark-haired and attractive answered the door.

"Yes?" she said.

"Is Dr Thomas home?"

"I'm sorry. Dr Thomas doesn't live here anymore. I'm her tenant."

"How long have you been living here?"

I was too abrupt, and my question brought the answer it deserved. After she told me it was none of my business and I apologized and explained the situation, she told me she'd been living there for six months. By this time Natalie reappeared.

"Why is Doctor Thomas's car in the garage?" she said.

After I apologized again, this time for Natalie's prowling, the tenant replied, "That's the odd part of the arrangement. She comes every night with her car and leaves it here, then gets on her motorcycle and goes off, comes back in the morning and picks up her car. Sometimes I hear her in the middle of the night; I guess when she has to go to the hospital."

"Did you ever ask her what it was all about?"

"No."

That was it. The woman didn't know anything else about Roberta or her habits. I told Natalie to go home, and we would talk in the morning.

The next day, Wednesday, with no patients, I was catching up on paperwork when Natalie reappeared. Now what?

"She still hasn't called or come in. Should I call the police?"

"Let me do it. I'll go over there when I finish here. They'll consider it early for a missing person bulletin on an adult."

"What about the tenant? Maybe she lied, and Dr Thomas was in there tied up or dead."

"Get hold of your imagination. Roberta walked out of here on her own. What about the last patient? Who was she?"

"Mrs Hudson."

Mrs Hudson had no intention, she said, of telling me what she discussed with the doctor. The doctor would likely explain when she returned. She hung up the phone. I was sure she had a shrewd idea of what triggered Roberta's departure.

An OPP detachment served as Arnprior's police force. I had no more luck there than with Mrs Hudson. The constable at the desk didn't intend to issue a missing person bulletin on a forty-five-year-old woman who left her office under her own steam.

I conceded his point. If Roberta returned from a personal crisis to find the whole town looking for her, she wouldn't be delighted with me.

Natalie came over to the office with a message. Mrs Hudson had called, upset, and wanted to speak to me right away and could I come over and talk with her. Of course, I could.

Arnprior has a warren of little streets near the river that wind up and down tiny hills. A few artists and some old families who occupied the same houses for generations live in the area. Mrs Hudson's house stood on a little dead-end street called Carss.

I parked in front of a larger two-story house clad in pale green aluminum siding, somewhat the worse for its many years of service, likely since the nineteenth century. Mrs Hudson opened the door as I took the few steps needed to reach her.

"Thank you for coming, Dr McPhail. I didn't know what else to do."

The upright old lady, usually quite fierce, I was sure, looked pale and shaken and clung to my hand.

"How can I help you, Mrs Hudson?"

"Oh, please, call me Mary."

She talked on and continued to apologize for bothering me as we walked into her front room. I was taken back twenty years to my own grandmother's house with its double parlour, overstuffed furniture and highly polished cabinets, footstools covered with needlework and large fern in the bow window. I almost expected to see my grandmother in her chair in the corner, reading one of her favourite mystery novels.

"Mary, try to tell me what's wrong? Are you ill?"

"Oh, no, it's not about me at all. It's my friend, Pearl. She's being blackmailed!"

Pearl told her a man called, threatening to tell her family she had a child out of wedlock, sixty years before, when she was eighteen. Her aunt raised her as Pearl's cousin.

"But surely everybody in the family knows about the child."

"Oh, yes, of course. That's not what upset Pearl. The man had details she told only to Dr Thomas. She is certain the information came from her."

I couldn't believe Roberta would break her patient's confidence. Could it have come from Natalie? But Natalie was not the one who ran away from the office. If Roberta thought the young woman was the source of information from her office she would have handled it.

"Did you tell this to Dr Thomas?"

"Yes, I did. I didn't tell you before because she asked me to keep it to myself until she discovered how the information leaked from her files."

"I'm glad you told me now. Dr Thomas grew up here. You knew the family?"

"Yes, I did. They lived in Braeside. I belonged to the Women's Institute with her mother and her aunt."

"Where did they live?"

"I might have it in an old address book."

Of course, she would, I thought, as she went off to find it. Old address books, cards, invitations, all the memories of a long life would be put away in the dressers and bookcases of her house.

"Here it is. I hope you can find her and clear all this up."

I promised her I would try. I wanted to pick up Natalie before I went knocking on any more doors. I suppose I should have called the police, but I expected to find Roberta and somehow hear a reasonable explanation for all of this. We drove to the address Mrs Hudson gave me.

When I knocked on the door in the small Braeside war-time house, it swung open slowly. I called out hello but got no reply.

"Can you go round back and check if the motorcycle is back there or anyone is outside?" I asked Natalie.

"Are you going in?"

"If no one answers, I think so."

I didn't want her in with me. I had a bad feeling about the smell that came at me through the open door.

I found him in the living room, his eyes staring at the ceiling. Middle-aged and a little overweight, he was no one I recognized.

He'd been dead at least a day. Rigor mortis had come and gone. Lividity stained his jaw and the underside of his neck. A wound at the back of his skull had oozed blood into the carpet where it pooled and gelled. Blood and hair adhered to the fender of a black woodstove. Had he fallen and hit his head? That would have taken quite a fall. No weapon visible.

Where was Roberta? I checked the upstairs bedrooms then ran back downstairs to keep Natalie from coming in. I met her at the door.

"Don't come in. There's a dead man in here. Go call 911. My cell is in the car."

Natalie turned and ran back to the car without a word.

I didn't say murder because I didn't know. Perhaps it had been an accident. Every step I took, Roberta seemed to be in deeper trouble.

When Natalie came back, we sat on the steps and waited for the police. Then we sat on the steps and waited for the detectives. We were still sitting on the steps when dusk fell. I got up and pounded on the door.

"What is it?" the young constable asked.

"Natalie and I are leaving," I said with more assurance than I felt. "We've waited for hours, and we're both tired and hungry. We gave you our addresses, and we will both be at work in the morning if you want to talk to us."

"Hang on, while I ask the detective."

Moments later the detective came to the door, asked us in, had Natalie look at the body. After I dealt with her faint, he wanted to hear our story, which I gave him as rapidly as an ICU report at two in the morning.

"So you were looking for this Dr Thomas. Why'd you enter the house?"

"The door swung open, and I thought the house belonged to Roberta, so I went in calling her name. Also the smell."

"Yeah, it was getting bad. Did the other woman come in the house at all?"

"No, I sent her around to look in the backyard."

After a few more questions, and after the coroner arrived and confirmed the man had been dead at least one day, the police let us go.

Thursday and Friday mornings were busy in the office. I didn't have time to think about Roberta until a patient mentioned her on Friday. Her disappearance had hit the newspaper.

A young couple from the nearby village of Calabogie came in with their new baby and their three-year-old son. The little boy cuddled under my left arm, watching the fish on my screen-saver, as I reassured the parents about their newborn. The father asked a question about Roberta as his wife loaded the baby into the car seat.

"Have they found the missing doctor yet?"

"Not that I've heard."

"I think I saw her yesterday, in the store where I work."

"Where do you work?"

"Sobey's in the village. I'm the produce manager," he said proudly.

"Did you call the police?"

"Yes, someone came out and looked around and asked the rest of the employees but no one else noticed her. I don't think he believed me. Her family had property up at Norway Lake, eh?"

"Did they?"

"So my grandmother said."

My ancestors had moved in and out of Calabogie several times over the last one hundred and fifty years. I spent my childhood going to school there, so I knew his grandmother. If anyone would know who lived where she would.

"I could ask her and call you back," he said.

"Thanks."

As they were leaving, the little boy hung back, reluctant to leave until he saw his favourite, the shark. Three and four-year-olds loved the screensaver, and always the shark was the hit.

Before I left for the morning, the father called back with his grandmother's directions, which included her statement that the land was beside my great-great-grandfather's property. I did know, but only because I found the homesteading document while doing genealogy research.

When I went across to tell Natalie about the lead on Roberta, she wanted to come with me, but she was still phoning patients. I asked her to call the detective and tell him about the farm at Norway Lake.

I drove out of Arnprior, crossed Highway 17 and took the road towards the village of White Lake. After the village, the road passed through a rock-cut and across a bridge, with breath-taking views of the Madawaska River, into the small crossroads hamlet of Burnstown. Resisting the temptation to stop and browse through the art galleries, gift and antique stores that filled the old buildings, I turned left onto the Calabogie Road.

Norway Lake Road ran north outside Calabogie, and I searched for landmarks after I caught my first glimpse of the lake.

The farm wasn't hard to find. The mailbox at the end of the long lane still read D. Thomas. I pulled up behind a black and chrome motorcycle. The farmhouse had been a log cabin, I thought, as I crossed the narrow porch. Another door off the latch. I pushed the door and called out. No answer.

A computer was open on the kitchen table, surrounded by files and a few books. A kettle sang away to itself on the stove. I called out again. Still, no answer and the kettle was about to boil dry. So I went in.

The documents on the table were personal—birth and adoption certificates, marriage certificates and even a few school records.

Odd, when I mentioned my hobby of genealogy, Roberta didn't tell me she was interested in it too.

The floorboards behind me creaked.

"Find what you were looking for, Anne?"

I jumped at the sound of her voice and struggled to keep the panic out of mine. She stood behind me, cradling a rifle in her arms, watching,

"Roberta, I'm so glad to see you. We were so worried when you disappeared."

She stared back at me with bleak dead eyes.

"Why were you looking through my stuff?"

Why was I? Because it was there and might tell me what happened.

"I was looking for you. Natalie asked for help after you left on Tuesday."

She prowled around the farmhouse kitchen, keeping the rifle aimed in my direction. This wasn't the woman I knew.

"He's dead. Do you know that?"

"Yes, I know that."

More prowling, touching objects, all the time watching me. I inched towards the door.

"Stop."

"It's time for me to go."

"No. You'll tell them where I am. They'll come for me."

Her words came in a sing-song, little girl cadence.

"We'll get people to help you."

"I killed him. I pushed him, and he fell and hit his head and he died."

The chilling words came in the same childlike tones. "Now, I have to kill you too."

"Of course, you don't have to kill me," I said.

Maybe if I were matter-of-fact, she would come around. "You didn't mean to kill him. I'll help you explain it to them."

She looked at me and shook her head. "They won't understand. You don't understand."

"Tell me."

"I loved him, but he used me. He used things I told him about the patients."

Her voice came stronger, more adult.

"He was blackmailing your patients?"

"Yes."

I heard a car stop on the bit of gravel driveway just outside the kitchen door. Roberta ranted on, telling me how much she loved him and how betrayed she felt. She didn't seem to notice the sounds outside. How I hoped Natalie had called the police and not come up here herself. I strained to hear the car doors open, but whoever was out there was being quiet.

"Why did you push him? Were you fighting about the black-mailing?"

"No. I told him what Mrs Hudson had told me. Even after that he grabbed me and tried to kiss me."

Horror-stricken, she stared at me, expecting me to understand, even though she had told me nothing. The door swung silently inward behind her.

"Police, Dr Thomas. Put down the rifle."

He had his gun in his hand.

Roberta turned around, pulling up the rifle, aiming at the police-man, releasing the catch on the safety.

His shot hit her in the chest. She was gone before she fell.

Days later, the funeral over, Natalie and I were sorting the charts in Roberta's office when Mrs Hudson knocked at the door.

"Dr McPhail, could I speak to you?"

"Certainly. Come back into Roberta's office. How can I help you?" I asked.

She perched on the edge of the visitor's chair. "I feel so responsible for this tragedy. If I hadn't told her about her family history, this would have never happened."

"I don't understand, Mrs Hudson. What did you tell her that upset her so?"

As I drove away from Arnprior towards my home in Bridgenorth, her reply ran through my mind like the lyrics to some country song.

"Oh, I thought you knew. The man she killed, who'd been her lover, was her twin, her brother."

DEATH IN FRENCH

Anne and Thomas visit Quebec City where a journey into a man's past puts Anne in danger. Published on Wattpad.

3

DEATH IN FRENCH

From the seventeenth floor of the Quebec City Hilton, Anne saw the great river shining in the sunset behind the battlements of Old Quebec. Below lay the gates of the city, now busy as people turned onto Rue Rene Levesque and into the rush hour traffic. In their assembling yard, the calèche drivers unhooked their horses from the old carriages and loaded the tired animals into vans for the journey back to their stalls. She was joining Thomas in the executive lounge for a drink and hors-d'oeuvres before they went out to a restaurant in the old city.

The lounge opened off the main floor and into a tiny reception area, just big enough for the concierge's office. The room beyond, however, contained several comfortable sitting areas and small tables and chairs. A largish alcove to the far left was reserved for smokers. Several people were standing at the drinks and food table to the right. Anne took her glass of white wine to a table at the window with its view of the majestic Second Empire architecture of the Parliament. One more night here and this will be "our" table, she thought.

The room was slowly filling up with people, some of whom she remembered from the evening before. A German-speaking couple sat the table behind her—he, a stooped, still trim eighty or so, she, perhaps a few years younger, and developing the type of pale frailty that elderly women do. A multilingual group took the round table across from her, dominated by a large man who moved in and out of three languages, odd for the American he seemed to be. Two women surrounded by shopping bags, relaxed on a couch and chattered in French while waiting for their husbands to join them from the convention.

Thomas arrived, and they collected drinks and murmured about their days, listening, in the pauses in their conversation, to the chatter around them. The group behind them planned a trip to Montmorency Falls. The old man walked by on his way, Anne supposed, to the washroom, leaving his wife with that uncomfortable air that women have who are unused to being at a table alone. A burst of excited French and sudden laughter came from the women on the sofa as their husbands joined them.

Something seemed out of place, though. At the corner of one of the sofas, Anne noticed a little movement under a table. Whatever it was, didn't seem to bother the young couple sitting there. Curious, Anne watched a little longer and was rewarded by the sight of a small boy—in the room strictly against the rules—perhaps four years old, creeping from the protection of the table and towards the alcove. The child stood up and stared into the alcove, quiet and alert the way children were when they saw something they didn't quite understand. His mother looked up, spoke to him urgently and he ran back to her. She tucked him under the table again.

The couple with the illegal small boy took advantage of the concierge's disappearance into the kitchen to hustle him out of the room, stuffing his treasures into a Snoopy backpack as they went. The old man shuffled back, picking up a newspaper from the sofa-table as he went by.

"Another glass of wine?" Thomas asked.

"No, I don't think so."

Thomas started to say something like, "shall we go", when a

woman, screaming, ran from the alcove into the arms of her husband. Anne could just make out the word "mort" from the torrent of French.

"I'd better go," she said.

But her medical services weren't needed. She identified herself, in her careful French, to the concierge. He pointed to the side of the alcove where a man's body lay back in a wingback chair. A tiny ribbon of blood twisted down his forehead from a circular wound. Anne didn't need to touch the body to know the man was dead, but she put two fingers on his carotid and waited the requisite minute before she nodded at the concierge and said "Mort," and then, "Sûreté".

She waited by the body until the concierge had returned then went back to Thomas. The little boy had left one of his drawings under the table.

"What happened?" Thomas asked.

"An assassination, I think. We're going to be stuck here for a while."

"In that case do you want another glass of wine before the cops show up?"

"I do."

The room had emptied by the time the police arrived. Anne and Thomas remained, sipping wine and watching the activity until the investigator got around to Anne. A tall man, who reminded Anne of Yves Montand in the way his jacket hung from his shoulders and his head thrust forward as he asked his questions, introduced himself as Inspecteur Lebrun.

After they had told him their names and why they were in Quebec City, he asked what they had witnessed.

"Very little," Thomas said. "We were about to leave when the lady started screaming. Anne went to see what she could do. I sat and waited."

"I verified that the man was dead, then came back here to wait for you," Anne said.

"Did anyone move in the direction of the alcove before the discovery?"

"Several people," Thomas said. "The washroom is that way, and there was some activity back and forth."

"Do you remember who?"

"No."

"I remember that the old man walked back there and a woman from the group sitting on the couch had gone before that. The staff went back and forth too." Anne said.

"Mueller," he said, consulting his notebook, "and Charbonneau. Did anyone leave before the event?"

"The couple with the little boy."

"Little boy? No children allowed in here, I thought."

"I know, but he was under his parents' table, colouring. He left one of his drawings behind."

"Where?"

The Inspector pulled on his gloves as he picked up the small paper under the table Anne pointed out to him. His face had an odd expression as he showed it to her.

The simple drawing showed a man-figure with his arm outstretched towards another sitting in a chair. The out-stretched arm held an object at the end, black, not pink as the boy had coloured the other hand.

"He saw it," Anne said. "I saw him staring into the alcove at one point. His mother called him to come back without going to see what had caught his attention."

"How old was he?"

"Judging by his drawing, between four and five years old."

"You can tell by the drawing?"

"Yes. We have a test, called the Goodenough Draw- a - Person Test, that identifies the ages at which children add details to their drawings."

"What kind of doctor are you?"

"A paediatrician."

"And do not many small boys draw pictures of "cops and robbers"?

"Sometimes, but—"

"A very young boy, Doctor and unlikely to be of any help. Do you think you could identify the parents?"

"I doubt it. I barely noticed them but I might be able to recognize the little boy."

"Perhaps the concierge. Do you remember anyone else moving about?"

"I think that big American at the table next to ours, went to the other room or the washroom," Thomas said.

Another mutter as he leafed through his notebook. "McTeague, he calls himself. Will you be here at the hotel for long?"

When they assured him that they would be there for three more days, the policeman stood up and moved to talk to the old couple at the next table.

As they walked out into the lobby, Anne said, "A small boy has eyes as good as anyone's."

"Not a credible witness in court, I suppose."

"Isn't it just a matter of getting a lead to the killer?"

"Not your problem, Anne. Try not to get involved this time."

Two days later the lounge was again open for breakfast. Anne sat enjoying a final cup of coffee. Most of the diners were new, but the Muellers and the group of Americans, McTeague among them, remained. At the buffet table, a lone man surreptitiously filled a bag with items.

That's the father of the little boy, Anne thought. She slipped out of her chair and followed him out of the lounge. She asked in French if she could speak to him about his little boy.

"We may speak English," he said.

"I believe your little boy saw that unfortunate event in the lounge."

"He did not," was the abrupt reply.

"He drew a picture of it, which the police have. He must be upset."

"I shall attend to the needs of my child, Madame."

He dismissed her concerns by turning his back and walking away. Anne flushed with embarrassment as she walked back to her table with her plateful of cheese and croissant.

Let it go, she scolded herself. Thomas was right. It wasn't her concern, and she'd given the police what she knew. Idly she watched the others in the room. The father of the boy finished filling his brown bag and walked to the door just as the concierge returned. Odd, she thought, as she watched Mueller take his wife's arm and pull her across the room. The group of Americans walked across in front of her, laughing and talking as they waited their turn in front of the desk. The old couple must have been unhappy with the information, because he slapped the table, flushed and angry before he turned and hustled his wife out into the lobby.

Anne waited a few minutes before she left the lounge. When she turned the corner to the elevators, the old man stood in her way.

"I wish to talk to you," he said in the precise English of the educated European.

"What can I do for you?"

"I wish to know the name of the man you spoke to at the buffet. My wife and I wish to give a present to the small child, who must be quite frightened by the events of yesterday."

"I'm sorry, but he didn't tell me his name."

"You must tell me."

Emotion suffused his face again as he sputtered the words out.

"I don't know it. Good day," she flung over her shoulder at him as she turned on her heel and retreated to the safety of the lobby. Mueller stared venomously at her as the couple walked across the lobby to the doors.

What could she do? That inspector wouldn't listen to something as thin as this. He would just tell her that the man was upset because he wasn't getting his way. And maybe that's all it was. She was probably suspicious because the man looked like a villain in an old war movie.

She picked up a cast-off tourist guide and tried to divert herself with the Arts section. The Picasso ceramics show was still here, and she wanted to see it. Thomas would be out of his first meeting soon. Perhaps they could go together.

From where Anne sat she saw the elevator doors, as they opened and closed, emptying the guests into the lobby to start their days of sightseeing or conference-going. The American group crowded around the car rental desk as they arranged for their trip to the Falls. Anne sat up when the family with the little boy walked to the front of the hotel. They must be out for the day, she thought, taking in the backpacks of father and son, and mom's capacious carryall.

Anne looked for the German couple. The woman was sitting in an upright chair, not far from Anne. The man was not in the lobby, but the little family crossed Rue Rene Levesque and the old man hustling after them before the lights changed. A cabby leaned on his horn as the old man reached the other side. A sudden fear that the man was going to kill the little boy propelled Anne across the room to the old woman.

"Where has your husband gone?" she demanded, watching fear play across the frail old face.

"I don't speak English." At least that was what Anne thought she said. She ran across the lobby and out the doors to the curb. The light was against her and the traffic very heavy on the workday morning. Far ahead the family walked up the hill to the Parliament buildings. There were police up there, she thought. Nothing would happen. He would have to follow them further.

She raced across as the lights changed, panting as she ran up the steep hill to the government building. The old man had disappeared, but the couple decided against the Parliament and were walking along the brick-paved street toward the St. Louis gate that guarded the approach to the Citadel. Soldiers, Anne thought. There were soldiers at the gate.

And then she saw him, stopped in a little park, sitting on the stone base of some heroic statue or another, casually pulling something from inside his coat. The early morning sun reflected off the object as he twisted it in his hands. She watched, horrified and unable to reach him in time as the American sighted along his arm.

But the old man was right behind him. He jerked at the gun-arm sending the bullet off target, falling aside to avoid the enraged blow aimed at his head. The gun flew out of the shooter's hand and landed at Anne's feet. The American took one step towards her, and then bolted towards the old town as the comforting sound of squealing brakes and sirens shattered the silence of the confrontation.

The old man sat, pale and shaking, on the base of the statue. She took his hand and felt his pulse, weak but steady under the soft old skin.

"You thought it was me?" he asked, his English more accented now.

"Yes, I did. Who are you? Who is he?"

"He is one of that vile new breed, the neo-Nazis, and the man he killed was his opposition in one of the South American countries. I cannot tell you which one. I was to meet with him today."

"And you are?"

Before he spoke, the paramedics arrived. They rolled up his sleeve to take his pulse and his blood pressure. Anne stared at the blue numbers on his forearm and then into the old man's eyes.

Anne looked down at the Kent gate from her room high in the hotel. The man, carrying his small son, and his wife, burdened now with the backpacks and bags, returned from their day of sightseeing. As they turned into the back entrance to the hotel, Inspecteur Lebrun stepped into their path. He would be telling them they were safe now; that the killer was in custody. They would never know that they owed their son's life to the old man, the Nazi hunter, who had answered her question by saying, "And now you know who I am."

HOMICIDE IN HALIBURTON

Anne and Thomas fly to an island in Haliburton County, Ontario for a business meeting that turns deadly. Published on Wattpad. A sequel to The Jewelled Egg Murders

4

HOMICIDE IN HALIBURTON

The bright-yellow plane circled lazily upwards into the darkening sky, leaving Thomas and me standing beside our luggage on the shore of the frozen lake. I was glad to be out of the plane and on the ground. Snow was moving in fast.

"I hear snowmobiles, I think," Thomas said.

He had a business meeting at this remote lake on the edge of Haliburton County. We had not had much chance to spend time together since we had met across the border in the small Vermont town of Culver's Mills. Thomas still called it home, although he spent more time in places like New York and Paris and Toronto. I hoped this weekend would help me see where our relationship was going.

The luggage loaded into the trailer behind one of the snowmobiles and helmets lodged on our heads, we began our sedate trip up the hill. A wide veranda wrapped around three sides of the two-story log cabin. Ten bedrooms at least, I thought.

"Have the other guests arrived?" I asked Ted, one of the drivers. He opened the massive oak front door and waved me through,

"Yes, ma'am. You're the last, and just in time too. Weather's coming in." The first few flakes of the approaching storm swirled through the doorway with us. Inside, the room opened to a vast living area, easily thirty by fifty feet, with walls constructed of massive old logs rising at least ten feet. Brightly-coloured rugs and shabby, overstuffed furniture warmed up all that exposed wood. Fires burned at each end of the room.

"Mr Beauchamp, Dr McPhail, welcome to Inverness."

The man holding out his hand in greeting was David McKnight, the manager of the lodge. He would have been called a butler fifty years ago, but the job remained the same. Long hair that hung free to his shoulders distorted that image, though.

"We've taken your luggage up to your rooms. Would you like to meet everyone, or go ahead upstairs?" McNight asked.

"Let's say hello before we go up," Thomas said.

Thomas hadn't told me much about the other people who were going to be at the lodge. I knew that one of them, Royce Barrington, had been a business rival for some time. Their host, Cooper Thwaite, headed an international conglomerate and wanted to involve either Thomas or Barrington or perhaps both, in a new enterprise. Barrington's son and daughter and their spouses had come for the weekend as well but were out cross-country skiing.

Cooper Thwaite was the quintessential Marlboro man: tall, weather-beaten (likely due to time spent on expensive golf courses, I thought unkindly, and it turned out unfairly), chiselled, handsome features and beautifully styled white hair. Only long fleshy ears and a gap between his front teeth marred the overall effect. His attractive wife, number two or three, judging by her age, was called Melinda.

Royce Barrington, on the other hand, wouldn't have been out of place in a small-town Rotary meeting. He was short, a bit heavy, and smiled all over his round face.

Andrea Barrington was and would remain wife number one, I thought. She seemed the sort of content, comfortable woman a man like Barrington would prefer.

"Thomas," Thwaite, "I am so glad you could bring Dr McPhail.

Welcome to Inverness, my dear," he went on turning to me. He held my hand a few seconds longer than custom demanded, although as I am short, and on the wrong side of forty, I suspected the hand-holding of being his habit with women.

The Barrington children came in and were introduced. They were all in their mid-twenties, cheerful and rosy from their adventures in the snow. I stood back watching the males in the room, including Thomas, circle around Melinda Thwaite. Andrea Barrington walked over and sat down beside me on a long sofa.

"Have you ever met Melinda and Cooper before, Anne?"

"No, I haven't," I said.

"I haven't seen you around at any of the functions in the city. Do you live in New York?"

"No, I live part of the time in Toronto and also in a country home in Ontario." I could see her interest in me fading. I supposed she thought she would never have to meet me after this weekend.

"Darling Melinda, surrounded by men as usual," she said. Her upper lip curled. "Don't be upset by Thomas, dear; he can't help it. None of them can."

She raised her glass of scotch and drained it. Comfortable Mrs Barrington had had more to drink than was good for her. Her daughter and daughter-in-law, Beth and Karen huddled near the closest fireplace, ignoring their husbands who formed part of the admiring group by Melinda.

Thomas came over to us and suggested we go up to our room and change for dinner.

"What's going on?" I asked when we were alone. "Quite a bit of tension down there."

"Tension? I didn't notice. Cooper wanted to talk to me his plans for our discussions this weekend. Who's tense?"

"All the ladies. I do believe they are all a little annoyed with our lovely hostess."

"Melinda? Beautiful as an angel and as thick as she is beautiful."

"Have you noticed it before, the tension when she's around?"

"All the time, honey, all the time," Thomas laughed.

Dinner went quite well, probably because the food was excellent, the wine plentiful and Mrs Barrington abstained. I enjoyed talking to her daughter, Beth, a historian who worked for the city of New York, and Beth's husband, Kevin Argyle, a city planner. Her son was in business with his father. His wife, Karen, had worked for a large charity before her marriage but was "too busy with her social commitments" to continue. She was also a few months pregnant and having a little trouble with the no-drinking rule. She sat next to the host, every move scrutinized by her mother-in-law across from her.

Melinda's companions were Brad Barrington and Kevin Argyle. If I'd been Andrea Barrington, it would have been my son I watched. He drank heavily and steadily and monopolized Melinda. I wondered if her elderly husband noticed. Karen certainly did.

After dinner Cooper, Thomas, Royce and Brad moved to the other end of the long room and sat around a low table spread with file folders and laptop computers. Cooper suggested bridge to the rest of us.

I played, but not very well, so left the table to the others, including Melinda who, to my surprise, wanted to play for stakes. I wondered if she was as thick as Thomas had joked. After watching for a while, I wondered off to look at the paintings and other objects around the room. Karen had disappeared at the first mention of cards.

The evening ended early, for me at least. Thomas' business meeting went on past midnight. When he came to bed, he curled up against me, snuggling his face into my hair.

"Sorry about this evening, dear heart. Cooper insisted."

"That's okay. I looked at Cooper's lovely pictures and then came upstairs to read."

Moments later, his breathing smoothed out, and he slept, but I was wide awake again. Knowing from long experience that sleep wouldn't come, I slid out of my side of the bed, put on a robe and started out to find the kitchen.

A pale glow from strip lighting on the stair-risers led the way downstairs. It was so cold that I thought they must turn the heating down at night. The kitchen lay to the right of the stairs through a heavy pine door. Earlier, I'd noticed that it swung smoothly for the tray-laden server, but when I pushed, it pushed back. Wind, not gale force, but strong gusts that swirled snow around the kitchen, piling it into corners, struck me when I forced my way into the kitchen.

Double doors led from the kitchen onto a patio. I could see in the glow from the automatic light in the refrigerator's ice dispenser that something large held one of them wide open.

The large object was Cooper, half-covered with snow, and lying in a pool of red. He was still warm to touch, but dead. Another body. Every time I went on vacation I stumbled across a corpse.

I pulled myself up from where I had squatted next to Cooper. The cold raced through me, and I shook, a leftover from mild PTSD. What to do now? I wondered where that manager went at night. He would be the logical person to take charge, seeing it was the host who had died. I didn't want to be the one to tell Melinda. Then I remembered Thomas.

I pulled open the heavy door, slipped through and let the wind slam it shut again. Better to keep that room as cold as possible for now.

Thomas was snoring when I came in, little flutters of breath that sounded like a tiny car revving up. Too bad to wake him, I thought.

"Thomas," I called.

He was instantly awake, one of those people who have no transition between sleep and awareness.

"What is it? What's the matter," he asked as he sat up and took my hands.

"I found Cooper's body in the kitchen."

47

I don't usually blurt out bad news—bad form for a doctor—but it seemed the only way.

"Heart?"

"No, a blow to the head, from what little I could see. I just made sure he was gone, and then came up to get you. I didn't know where to find that McKnight fellow."

"I think he has rooms in the other wing."

Thomas was up and dressed in sweatshirt and pants by the time I finished giving him all the details of what I"d seen. He thought perhaps I wanted to stay in the room, but there was no way I was spending any time alone anywhere in the house except the bathroom until the cops got there. I was sure Cooper had been murdered.

No bright dawn this morning, just a gradual increase in the light outside. The snow had fallen all night heavily, and didn't look to be easing. The wind continued to howl around the eaves, and an occasional loud explosion from the bush marked the death of a tree as its branches became too heavily laden.

David McKnight and Thomas carried Cooper's body to an unheated shed behind the house. Yes, we knew the rule about not moving the body, but we all had to eat, and that kitchen was filling up with snow. McKnight seemed to know what he was doing because he took picture after picture with his digital camera before he and Thomas carried Cooper's body away.

The rest of us clustered at one end of the living room, drinking coffee while we waited for the kitchen to warm up enough to cook in. McKnight had told us that most of the staff lived out, at a village about ten miles away and were not expected in because of the storm. He would try to organize some breakfast when he had finished contacting the police.

"McKnight didn't say what kind of accident Cooper had. Do you know?"

Royce Barrington turned from where he stared out the window at a landscape obscured by blowing snow, and looked at me.

"I think I will wait until David and Thomas come back to talk about it," I replied.

"Why?"

"Because I think we should all hear it together."

I snuggled further under a warm blanket that Beth Barrington had given me when she found me shivering on the sofa, and tried to ignore the glares from everyone else.

"Come off it, lady," snarled Brad. He and his father loomed over me. It must have looked as menacing as it felt because Thomas shouted at them as he came in with David.

"What the hell do you guys think you're doing? Back off."

"What the fuck happened to Cooper? The doctor here won't tell us. We have a right to know." Rage twisted Brad's face into an ugly mask.

"Only Melinda has a "right to know", I said, "and I've already told her. I also have to tell the police. Don't tell me what I have to do. I've been in this situation before." I turned to Thomas who sat down beside me and took my hand.

David interrupted before Brad could start again. "I can't reach the police at the moment, folks. The CB radio only has a range of five miles, and I can't raise anyone. The phones are down. Our generator will last about 10 hours with the fuel that I have on hand, so I'm going to cut back on the rooms I put the power into—especially this one—and bring in some oil lamps. We'll keep the power for cooking and heating."

He left for the kitchen, lucky guy. I'd rather have left the room too.

"You mean we're stuck in this hole with a murderer!" Melinda's high-pitched, whining voice came from the stairs.

"Murderer!"

"Who said anything about a murder?"

"I want to get out of here. Kevin, let's get a snowmobile and go." Beth's voice rose above the others as she pulled at her husband's arms.

Melinda glided into the room, fully dressed, fully made up with every hair in place, looking every inch a merry widow except for the fear in her beautiful eyes. "Anne and Thomas said he was murdered. One of you killed him."

"You are the one who benefits from his death." Andrea's comfortable voice had taken on quite a nasty edge.

"That's where you're wrong. I got a settlement when we married, and he put everything else out of my reach. And I loved Cooper, no matter what you might think."

I muttered to Thomas that we were going to need to feed the beasts and left to help David in the kitchen.

As I buttered toast and stirred scrambled eggs, I noticed that David and Thomas had blocked off the end of the kitchen. I supposed they hoped to keep some evidence for the police.

"Have you worked for the Thwaites very long?" I asked David.

"I've worked for Mr Thwaite for five years. I don't work for her at all, except for when we are up here. Usually, I'm a personal assistant at the office."

The conversation had turned to business when I went back to the breakfast table.

"Thomas, did you and Cooper agree last night?" Melinda asked.

"Does that matter right now?"

"I think so. He told me that if he chose your company, Barrington would go under. There are a lot of Barringtons here. Maybe one of them thought that I would be more likely to choose their company if he were dead."

"I doubt that anyone here believed you would be running the company if Cooper died," Andrea said.

"No one knew about the prenup, except David, so any one of you could have thought that," Melinda insisted.

"Frankly, dear, no one would have thought Cooper dumb enough to leave you in charge of breakfast, let alone a multi-million dollar company," Andrea said.

"Leave it alone, Andrea," her husband ordered. "I would like to know the answer to that question, though, and I would like to know the effect on your company if he had chosen mine," he asked Thomas.

I could feel Thomas's hand tense in mine and watched the colour rise in his face as he answered, "We did come to a tentative agreement after you left us, but it included both of us. I'll show you the outline if you like. It's a waste of time now that he's dead. We'll have to wait for the executor and the board now."

"Wait! I can't wait too long. You know that, Tom."

"I know that. We'll have to see how Cooper left the company. Perhaps it's in a trust for Melinda."

"No," said Melinda. "He told me that what he gave me when we married is all I would get and even that's all in a trust."

"So you say," Brad Barrington said.

"If you think that I inherited the company, maybe you killed him. You've always had a thing for me. Maybe you thought you could leave your little wife to her society affairs and marry me and the company after he was dead." Melinda turned her lovely and not so vacant eyes on Brad.

"You bitch," screamed Karen, "as if Brad would leave me for a brainless idiot like you. Tell her, Brad, tell her what you think of her."

The Barrington seniors and Beth interrupted, trying to calm the situation. Melinda, I noticed, sat back in her chair, with a Cheshire cat smile on her face as the arguments raged around her.

"Did Cooper have any children?" I asked Thomas. The question came out louder than I intended in a lull in the conversation. A deadly little silence ended when Thomas answered no.

"Not any legitimate ones anyway," said Andrea.

"What's that supposed to mean," Melinda asked.

"He did have a life before you, dear, and he didn't marry all his ladies."

"What would be the position of an illegitimate child," I asked.

"Depends on a lot of things, I think," Thomas replied, "especially how the will was written, but I think all children have rights."

By this time, breakfast was over. Thomas and I sat in a remote corner of the room. I thought over the various motives that had surfaced during that ghastly meal. Barrington's financial trouble could have inspired one of them to think the chances were better with Melinda. Brad, maybe, in spite of what his wife thought. We only had Melinda's word for it that she was cut out of the will. Maybe she thought her husband was tired of her and ready to move on to wife number four.

And what about other children. There were other people in the house. Who was Kevin Argyle, and what about the pair in the kitchen? One or both of them could have killed him. David said Mike was a stranger. They seemed to be friendly for guys who had just met. Even Beth Barrington was a possibility.

I looked around the room. The Barringtons were huddled together at the breakfast table, but Melinda had disappeared.

For the rest of the morning, I read, and Thomas napped. The Barringtons moved restlessly between their rooms and the living room, all except for Royce who slept soundly on a sofa matching the one Thomas was on. The storm raged on outside. Snowstorms that went on for days were rare in Ontario, but this was day two with no sign of it letting up.

At lunchtime I suggested we all help ourselves in the kitchen. As I finished washing dishes, and how I got elected chief of that chore I didn't know, I could hear screaming approaching. Karen burst through the door, still screaming until Andrea grabbed her and shook her.

"Melinda's dead. I knocked on her door to talk to her, and she's lying on the floor," she gasped when she had regained control.

"How do you know she's dead?" I asked. I dried my hands and started out of the room.

"She's pale and still and lying on the floor."

"Where's her room?"

"I'll show you," offered David as he followed me out the door and up the stairs.

Melinda and Cooper had separate rooms. Melinda's was surprisingly austere, but perhaps they hadn't spent enough time here for her to bother with décor. A white iron double bedstead stood against one wall. Melinda lay on one corner of the pale-blue bedcover that had been dragged or thrown onto the floor. She was dead and had been for some time. Her skin was cold, and I could see the dark stain of lividity that spread along her underarms. The arm had stiffened, so rigor mortis had set in but hadn't had time to leave again. As far as I could remember that meant it had been several hours since the time of death. She was face down, but I could see dark purple marks around her neck. Strangled, I thought, and by a large pair of hands.

David stood in the doorway, keeping the others out of the room.

"Can you see what killed her," he asked.

"Strangled, I think."

"What in God's name is going on here?

"I don't know, but we're leaving this just as we found it," I answered as I walked past him out the door and into the crowd in the hall.

"Is she dead?" Thomas asked as he put an arm around my shoulders.

"Yes. Let's go downstairs."

The group around the table was past fighting and accusations. Everyone was afraid, or at least all but one. I told them that Melinda was dead but didn't go into any details about what I had found.

"What the hell? That's all you're going to say? She's dead. We could see that. How did she die?" Brad Barrington again, angry and blustering.

"Strangled, and that's all I'm going to say until I talk to the police. One of you is a murderer," I said wearily, "and the rest of you shouldn't know what it looked like in there."

"But I know," Karen protested.

"Keep it to yourself," I said.

"What are we going to do?" Beth said.

"Stay together, wait for the storm to stop, call the police," Thomas answered.

And that's what we did, moving to the other end of the room, each little group staking out its space and staring uneasily at the others. I like to draw, but I thought that would cause a stir in the current atmosphere, so instead, I looked at each face as though planning a sketch.

Karen's ultra-thin modern face had started to fill out and soften with her pregnancy into her fourth month. She seemed uncomfortable with me looking at her so I moved on.

The Barrington children both had a strong resemblance to their mother. She must have been attractive when she was younger before alcohol had swollen and distorted her face. I'd thought of it as comfortable, but now she looked boozy and aged to me. Beth and Brad shared her short, upturned nose, round blue eyes and broad jaw.

Kevin Argyle's crooked nose dominated his sharply etched face with its tight skin and angular cheekbones. He was sitting across from David McKnight. I hadn't looked at David before; all that hair kept getting in the way. He must have felt me staring at him because he turned and flashed me a gap-toothed grin and thumbs-up sign. As he turned back to talk to Kevin, I had a sudden flash of what?— recognition, I suppose. Those large fleshy ears and that space between the front teeth were those of the dead man. Ears can be a strong genetic trait, even thought as individual as fingerprints. Perhaps it was just a coincidence. Surely in all the time that they had lived together, someone had noticed the resemblance.

Time for me to retreat to the bathroom to think. My mother had always told me to be careful about my face because my thoughts showed. Better to be alone while I decided what to do. I told Thomas where I was going and walked up the stairs. Behind me, I could hear David telling Mike that he was going to try the radio again.

I hadn't decided whether I would tell the others what I thought when Karen called to me through the door. "Anne, are you almost finished? I feel sick."

She was a big woman, and the force of her attack drove me back into the room. Her hands reached for my throat as I tried to get my arms up to protect it. As I twisted away from her, my elbow hit the bridge of her nose, and she howled in pain and rage. Now she had her knee on my chest and was pulling back her fist. I couldn't breathe, and I couldn't fight her any longer.

"No, you don't." Thomas had his arm around her neck and dragged her off me and out into the hall. Then he was with me, holding me.

"Where is she?" I asked when I could speak again.

"Kevin and Dave have her."

Thomas thought I should lie down, but one stupid mistake was enough. I wasn't going to be alone again until I was back in my little house in Bridgenorth, even if Karen was under lock and key.

The faces of the remaining Barringtons turned toward us, silent and pale.

"Why?" Brad's question. "Why?"

David McKnight answered as he came back into the room. "She had an affair with Cooper last year. That baby she's carrying is his. When he wouldn't leave Melinda to marry her, she killed him. She killed Melinda so that only her baby would be left to inherit the company."

"That's still true," I said.

"No, Cooper left the company to me and dealt specifically with any minor children living at the time of his death. His will gives me the responsibility for looking after their financial needs through a trust he set up in the will."

"How many are there?" I asked, fascinated by this Victorian approach to parental responsibility.

"Two boys and a little girl as well as Karen's baby if it lives."

"Why did she attack me?"

"She said you were staring at her. She thought you knew what she had done."

"Why did he leave the company to you?" Thomas asked.

"I'm his son."

Later that day, the storm cleared, and we were able to contact the O.P.P. Thomas and I flew out the next day on the little yellow plane. I looked down at the lodge and David McKnight's solitary figure, diminishing as we spiralled up into the bright blue sky.

My feelings for Thomas had grown stronger, but I wasn't sure whether the emotion was love or gratitude for saving my life. A problem to be solved later. He took my hand as the plane levelled off and he sank back into his seat and closed his eyes.

MURDER IN AN ORIENTAL GARDEN

Anne and Thomas fly to Vancouver to attend a business conference. Anne's visit to the Dr Sun Yat-Sen Garden leads her to yet another dead body.

5

MURDER IN AN ORIENTAL GARDEN

*T*he hotel car stopped in front of a building in Chinatown.
"Walk through," the driver said. "The Garden is beyond the gates."

The guard at the door told me I was too early. The tour would start in forty minutes in the Scholar's room, but meanwhile, he welcomed me wait there or walk in the garden. I'd come alone while Thomas was at a meeting; there would be ghosts to deal with. Michael and I honeymooned in Vancouver and returned for our anniversary the year he died. That was three long years ago, and I had found Thomas, but I wanted to be alone in the garden.

I had my hand on the door when a man burst through, shoving me out of the way. I fell against the guard, knocking him into the wall. We helped each other up, and the man who hit us slowed to a fast walk through the lobby and on out. His gait stuttered with a limp and a lurch on the left, which disappeared when he slowed down.

I would tell the police he wore a Canucks jacket and a blue ball cap. Eyewitnesses are poor at recalling details, but I was certain about the jacket, and the gait.

But that would be later. Right now my back hurt where I had hit the doorjamb. I walked through and into a Chinese landscape.

I rested on a low wall overlooking the jade-green water of a pond. Across from me rose Yun Wei Ting, a mountain in miniature capped with a pavilion.

When the time came to join the group in the Scholar's garden, I noticed a window in the wall that looked out on a minimalist garden — a weeping tree, two plump urns and beyond them a stream. Something lay in the opening in a low wall enclosing that area of the garden. In a moment, I realized I was looking a foot, in a blue running shoe.

The guide came back with me.

"He's bleeding," he said.

A man lay behind the low wall, blood staining his shirt and the soil around him. Bleeding was the wrong word. His heart had stopped pumping; the blood had pooled and thickened. The face, pale as the concrete of the wall beside it was familiar to me. I'd seen him at breakfast that morning at our hotel.

The guide called 911 on his cell. I walked back to the bench under the window and waited.

The investigator who took my statement thanked me and seemed a little bored when I told him what I knew. And that was all, I thought, as I took a taxi back to the Sutton Place Hotel where we were staying.

Thomas said I was becoming a magnet for violent crime. I had seen more than my share in the previous years from Vermont to Bermuda to Spain. But those had been more intimate crimes, involving familiar people. This was, or so I thought, random city crime, with no personal connection to Thomas or to me.

"Did you say you'd seen him before?" said Thomas, as he pulled a rain-jacket out of the closet.

"At breakfast. He sat at a table in front of the window across from me. A woman joined him for coffee."

"His wife?"

"If she were, they weren't getting along. They were angry. Her voice started to get a little shrill, and he hushed her. She said, and this I heard distinctly, "Don't try to stop me, Anderson. I won't let you ruin me."

She pushed the table away, so hard it rattled the cups, and marched across the room and on out.

"Anderson?"

He pulled a glossy brochure out of his conference folder. "Is this the man?" He showed me a picture, and when I nodded, he went on, "Anderson Wetley. He's the CEO of Wilderness Sands, and the keynote speaker this evening."

I called the number the detective had given me and left a message giving Wetley's name, and business. And that, I thought, as I clicked off the phone, was that.

The hotel loaned us an over-sized black umbrella as we left for Queen Elizabeth Park and lunch. First, we visited the triodetic dome of the Floral Conservatory. A fan of sci-fi on television would recognize it as a stand-in for an alien city on Stargate SG1. We needed the umbrella, as we ran through a sudden downpour to reach the door.

The glass and steel beehive opened up to a tropical paradise, with butterflies, birds, fish in the central pool and thousands of bromeliads, palms— one or two reaching the roof of the dome— and flowers everywhere. We wandered through, not stooping to read the soon-to-be-forgotten botanical names, but enjoying the sultry atmosphere. As we rounded a bend in the path, a raucous "hello" came from somewhere overhead. A gorgeous white cockatoo, called Charlie, according to the brochure, regarded us from a high branch. He repeated his greeting.

" Hello, Charlie," we called up to him. Satisfied, he flew off.

"It's time for lunch," Thomas said, glancing at his watch.

We left the dome and turned right towards the restaurant. We walked across the rain-slicked paving stones, watching the servers drying the tables and bringing cushions out for the chairs. The winds that had blown away the rain-clouds picked up leaves and pushed them against the stone wall surrounding the terrace. Sunshine lit the peaks of the five mountains visible from the table that we claimed.

The woman I had seen at breakfast sat at the table beyond ours. I couldn't see the face of her companion, but his hand stretched across the table, holding hers. She nodded, and the man stood up to leave. He left the terrace and hurried towards the parking lots. His gait was unsteady on the still-wet stones, and I wondered if he had too much wine at lunch. Then I remembered.

"That was the man who shoved me," I exclaimed to Thomas, as I pushed back my chair and ran after him.

Thomas shouted behind me, but I raced towards the parking lot when I lost sight of the man ahead. A car exited the parking lot and drove straight towards me. Beside me, the road fell off into a ditch and then a hedge. I threw myself down the slope as the car hit the sidewalk where I'd been standing. I could hear Thomas and then others yelling, and the car speeding up. I was afraid it was turning around to come for me again, and I scrabbled at the rain-slicked bank trying to climb towards the hedge.

"Annie, I'm here."

Thomas grasped my shoulders and pulled me to him.

"Are you hurt?"

"No, I don't think so," I whispered as I clung to him. "How did he know I was behind him?"

"I think the woman called him or texted him."

Someone called the police. We told the officers what we knew and where we were staying and returned to the hotel.

We walked through the mahogany doors of the hotel into the beautiful lobby. I was mud-spattered and wind-blown and wanted nothing more than a hot shower, but as we stood at the elevators, the concierge and another man came up to us.

"Inspector Bird of the Vancouver Police wishes to speak to you," the concierge said, and drifted away, duty done.

"Perhaps we should talk in our suite," Thomas said.

"Certainly." Inspector Bird, tall and lithe, with high cheekbones, joined us in the elevator and on up, saying nothing more.

The silence was uncomfortable, but I made it to our rooms without breaking into it. We sat down in the sitting room of the suite. The policeman chose a chair facing the door, with his back to the wall. We sat side by side on the sofa.

"I think you've had some difficult experiences since you arrived in Vancouver, Dr McPhail?"

"Yes, you could say that."

"Could you go over the events for me?"

I started with the ride to the Oriental garden and ended with Thomas pulling me from the ditch.

"Why did you go after the man?"

"An impulse. I recognized his walk, but I wanted to see his face. Thomas and I had identified the man who died and thought there might be a connection with the conference. The woman ate breakfast here in the hotel with the rest of us."

I stopped chattering as Thomas squeezed my hand. Wait for the questions that meant.

"And did you see his face?"

"No. We haven't looked for the woman in any of the conference material either."

I picked up Thomas' conference folder and leafed through the pictures, but didn't find a picture of her.

"I'll attend one of the spousal events. Perhaps I'll see her there," I offered.

"No more chasing," the detective ordered.

"Okay."

* * *

I signed up for a tour of the University of British Columbia and its gardens. A small group met the next morning for a breakfast meeting and slide show. Breakfast was served at scattered tables in a room dominated by a tall mahogany bar. Mirrors reflected the space and cut-crystal vases filled with flowers decorated the linen-draped tables. I took a free chair at a table towards the rear of the room.

The three other women introduced themselves and told me who their husbands were. I suppose that was so I could place myself in the pecking order. I admit that I said I was there with Thomas Beauchamp and mentioned his firm.

"I'm sorry. I missed your first name, Mrs Beauchamp," one said.

"My name is Dr Anne McPhail."

I looked around at the other half-dozen tables, maybe twenty people in all. None of them was the woman from the restaurant.

I was deciding whether or not I would go on the tour when another woman hurried in from the lobby. I recognized her as the woman I had seen at breakfast, the one who argued with Anderson Wetley.

"Trust Boothe, always an entrance," murmured one of the women at my table.

"Once an actress, always an actress," sniped another.

"Who is she?" I said.

"That's Boothe Walters. Her husband, Jackson Walters, is Chairman of the board of Wilderness Sands."

Wilderness Sands. Wetley, the CEO of that company died in the garden and this woman, Boothe, was the wife of the Chairman of the same company. She was also the woman who had threatened Wetley at breakfast, and the one who held the hand of the man who tried to kill me.

I drank another coffee and waited for the signal to leave. I kept hearing Detective Bird's admonition in my head. No more chasing, he said.

Going on a garden tour wasn't chasing, I decided, forgetting the woman had seen me.

"Do you think she's coming on the tour in those clothes?" said one of the others, staring at Boothe.

"I don't think so," said another.

The group leader, seated at Boothe's table, stood up and announced that the bus was waiting. When we climbed into the bus, Boothe was nowhere to be seen.

I knew the many distinct landscapes of the gardens at UBC, featured for many years on a gardening programme on the CBC. My favourite was a rock wall, with its crevices and cavities filled with tiny plants, part of the Alpine Garden. Soon we were walking along a pathway through a miniature alpine landscape. The narrow path winds past the rock wall. I lingered for a moment to take photographs of tiny lichens, glowing with minute flowers. I was intent on focussing my camera when she spoke to me.

"Why did you chase Blair?"

Startled, I almost dropped my camera as I swivelled to look her. It was Boothe, her face red and a crooked vein in her forehead purple and swollen.

"Who?"

"You saw him at the Chinese garden, and you chased him at lunchtime. Tell me the truth," she demanded as she took a step toward me. I backed up, but she moved closer.

"Truth about what? Who are you?"

"You know."

I backed away again, taking some of the precious lichens with me. Now I was around the corner and almost in sight of the main path.

"Who is Blair?"

Maybe if I asked her enough questions, I could distract her.

"My husband's assistant. You had to be there that morning. No one is ever there that early."

Rage contorted her lovely features, and she lunged towards me. I swung my camera and hit her on the side of the head and ran. I slipped on the pebbled path and bounced off a piece of granite at the main walk, but kept going towards the entrance. I'm a runner, but so was she, and she had longer legs. Her footsteps grew closer.

A man stepped out of a small copse of trees and stood in the pathway, pointing a gun at us. I stopped so fast Boothe ran into me, and we both went down. I was sure the next sound I heard would be the shot before I died.

But the sounds were of handcuffs being closed around Boothe's wrists and a voice reciting her rights.

"Do you need a hand, Dr McPhail?" said the same voice.

"Yes, no, I think I broke my wrist when she fell on me."

He helped me up and told me he was a police detective. We inspected my wrist, the left, bent at an impossible angle and swelling.

He explained to me, as we waited for Thomas and Inspector Bird, that he had been following Boothe.

* * *

A few hours, a wait in an ER and a cast later and Thomas and I sat with Inspector Bird in the living room of our suite.

"Why did Blair kill that man?" I said.

"He was to be the keynote speaker tonight. He intended to denounce his company and the industry for its cavalier attitude towards the environment. And he was going to use Wilderness Sands own facts and figures to do it. The bottom would fall out of the company's share price. Boothe convinced Blair, her husband's assistant, that Anderson was a threat to her husband and he would ruin him. She claims she didn't know he would kill Anderson. She couldn't tell us fast enough; she was that eager to make a deal."

"Were they lovers?"

"No, it's Jackson Walters he loves. When we told him she was talking, he told us what she had said, how she had convinced him, and he has tapes."

"Will she get her deal?"

"No. She'll go down with him."

The inspector left, and Thomas made me a drink, and we stood together at the window. The sunset stained the city towers and the mountain peaks in hues of violet and orange.

"How many times is that you've almost been killed?" he asked.

"Too many," I said and took another sip of my drink.

"I think you need to learn karate or kickboxing or something," he said, "or I'm going to keep you locked in your condo in Toronto and only let you out with an armed guard."

"Karate it is," I promised and snuggled back into his arms, only just missing his drink with my cast.

THE SECRET

Delving into one's own past can dig up secrets best left undisturbed.

6

THE SECRET

*J*an and I sat in our mother's home—a pause in clearing away Mom's life.

"What are we doing here, Diana? Can't this wait until tomorrow or next week or next month? What am I doing here anyway? You're the executor. The whole place is yours."

She waved her hand, her gesture encompassing the tidy room with its stiff, uncomfortable chairs and walnut tables, three of them, tops obscured by pictures in sterling silver frames and collections of crystal animals.

"No. The whole place is yours. I get the country house; you, this one. Do you want to keep anything?"

"I... I can't stay long to help you. You know the way Jim is."

She turned her sharp eyes to take in the room, but she wouldn't be counting dollars. She wasn't the type.

"Why do you let him get away with that control stuff?"

"What choice do I have?"

"You have one now."

"What?"

"This house, the contents, the insurance. You'll net a million or so. Leave him."

Jan sat back in the overstuffed chair she always chose, tucked up her legs and hugged her arms to her chest.

"You're serious? A million dollars. What's your share?"

"Same."

"Will you stay with William?"

I glanced up from the documents in my lap. "Of course. Why not?"

"So I can be alone but you can't?"

Always the competition.

"William doesn't try to control my life."

"You don't understand Jim."

I'd had enough of the familiar, endless argument and held up the key. "Do you remember what this is for?"

"How would I? Where did you find it?"

"In the box on Mom's silver chain."

"Maybe it's for the cupboard under the stairs?"

The oak stairs led up to our childhood bedrooms.

"Should we open it?" Jan's voice trembled and she burrowed deeper into the chair.

"I can do that later if you like."

"No. Why did she always lock the door?"

"Perhaps it started when we were little, and she didn't want us to get shut in. Remember the cellar."

The cellar. Locked inside for half-a-day with the spiders and the mice and the dark. Jan had been only six years old.

"Please don't talk about it."

I fit the key into the lock. It turned with no noise, no harsh metal protest from years of inactivity.

"What's there?"

"A box."

Stickers plastered on all sides warned Private and Fragile, and This Isn't Yours. I turned the contents out on the coffee table.

Baby clothes, for a boy. None for over six months. A pair of tiny brown shoes. A manila envelope.

"Whose clothes were these?" I asked. Not Jan. Maybe Mom's ghost, hanging around to see what we would do now.

I opened the envelope. One of those identikits, the sort parents, filled out in case their child was kidnapped. A print in ink of a tiny footprint. A birth certificate, a sheaf of letters from lawyers, a court document.

"A child, a boy."

"Whose child?"

"Mom's."

"What happened to him?"

"She gave him up when she was sixteen years old."

"So we have a brother."

What she'd always wanted: an older brother.

"Or a half-brother."

"Do you think she kept track of him?"

Jan still hunkered down in the chair. She shook her head no when I offered her the documents.

I searched the bottom of the box. A business card poked out from under a flap.

"There's a card from a private detective."

"So she looked for him?"

"I suppose so."

"Would we have to share the money?"

"No."

My field was corporate, not general law, but I was sure the will couldn't be overturned. My partner did good work.

* * *

Ten days later I took the elevator to the fifth floor of a drab brick building in midtown, the kind in which ancient dust lurked in the corners and chewing gum that used to be pink stuck to the floors. The sign beside the door read Peter Jenkinson, Private Investigation.

"You did some work for my mother before she died," I said. "Why?"

"I can't tell."

"Here is the death certificate and a copy of the will, my identification. I'm a lawyer, Mr Jenkinson. All my ducks are in a row."

"She said not to tell her daughters."

"She died too quickly to destroy her information. We found nothing from you. Did you report to her? Did she pay you?"

"Yes, cash. I reported, but she didn't want her copy."

"Did you find him?"

"Yes."

* * *

Three weeks later I got off a plane in Toronto and took a cab from the waterfront to small hotel off Bloor Street. Jan met me at the door of the two-bedroom suite.

"Jim let you come?"

"The money," she said and grinned. "What shall we do?"

"Make an appointment."

* * *

The bell above the door, tinkling, announced our entrance, and the store's antiquity. A young woman—long hair, ankle-length patterned skirt, gold-rimmed glasses—smiled and welcomed us to the bookstore.

"We have an appointment with Mr Sabato."

She sent us back through the store, following a path of checkered linoleum in grey and white. We passed books heaped on small tables, on stools, on grocery crates and on the shelves that filled the wall space, including the three feet between the door frame and the ceiling, into a room lit by a single window at the rear, to a desk in the corner.

"Mr Sabato, I'm Diane Anderson, my sister Jan Woolich."

He stood up, and when the light hit his face, I had no doubt. The slightly crooked nose and square jaw mirrored my sister's.

"What can I do for you?"

He cleared books from chairs that he dragged in front of his desk.

"Sit, sit."

"We came to discuss our mother with you."

"Your mother?"

"Yes. We have reason to believe that she was your mother, too."

"Another one. You have to leave now. I'm tired of these people turning up, claiming to be my half-brothers or half-sisters. What is wrong with you people? I had a perfectly good mother of my own. I don't need to hear about yours."

His square jaw jutted out, and his face turned an alarming shade of purple.

"Were you adopted, Mr Sabato?" I said again.

"No."

"We have some documents that say otherwise."

"Documents? No one else had documents. Gimme."

I passed over what we had. He snatched them from my hand, leaned back in his chair and started reading.

"Who's this Jenkinson?" he said after a few moments.

"A private detective our mother hired. Did a woman called Karen Meeks ever come to see you?"

"Yes, she was one of them. I remember her because she was the only one who claimed to be my mother."

"You sent her away?"

"No, I said I would do a blood test after she promised to include me in her will if I was her son."

"Did you do the test?"

"No. She never came back."

"When was this?"

"Two months ago."

"She had a stroke. She died six weeks ago."

He shifted his gaze to a picture on a bookcase, of a woman and a little boy. "So nothing in the will, then?"

"Nothing. Will you do the blood test?"

"No. No money, no test."

"Mr Sabato—"

He held the door open for us, and we walked back down the linoleum path.

"She said something about "the bastard doctor"."

His voice, pitched too loud, stopped us.

"What 'bastard doctor'?"

"No clue. She said it was all his fault."

We turned into the Starbucks on the corner and sat with lattes.

"Who was Mom's doctor?"

It was the only sentence Jan had uttered since we walked into the bookstore.

"That old guy, Billings. He died last month, too. I'll talk to the executor."

* * *

The doctor's executor, his grandson, was unaware, so he said, of the requirements that patients or their estates have access to records, but at least he hadn't burned them. The doctor stored the oldest in the carriage house behind his Victorian house.

"Help yourself," his grandson said.

Mom's records weren't in the alphabetically arranged files. The old doctor kept family files, everyone from grandparents to grand-nieces collected in one accordion folder. When I finished the Knewlys—Mom's family—I tried the Meeks. Nothing. I talked to the grandson again.

"My mother's file isn't there."

"Perhaps he sent it to her new doctor?"

"She didn't go to anyone after he died. She didn't like doctors. Do you have files anywhere else?"

"The red files. He kept those in a box in his room, but we haven't cleared it out yet."

"Can I look at them?"

"You can look at your mother's if you find it."

He was coming a little late to the privacy issues, but he brought down the bankers box, marked with the same sort of Do Not Open, Private stickers that Mom's box had.

I counted twenty files, marked with names I recognized—Mom's childhood friends, most of them. Why had he kept them separate? I wrote down the names when the grandson got bored with watching me turn over papers in my mother's file, reading every one, and left the room, mumbling something about tea.

One of the other files belonged to my brother-in-law's mother. I hurried through it, looking for what had become a gnawing suspicion, and there it was—a pregnancy. She was married at the time. What was she doing in the same box with my mother, if the pregnancy were the link? Not a box of the unwed mothers in his practice.

The grandson—Malcolm—still fussed in the kitchen. I checked another chart—another pregnancy, again an unwed mother. No fathers were listed, except for Jim's.

I'd read five charts by the time I heard him clanking back with the tea: all young women, sixteen or younger, all pregnant, all without naming the father, and all in this single file. All their subsequent pregnancies were included too. Perhaps it was just an obstetrical file? But there were only twenty altogether. Undoubtedly he attended more than twenty pregnancies in a fifty-year career and more than twenty unwed mothers. What made these women unique?

After I finished the tea, I thanked him and got up to leave. He shook my hand at the door. The evening light, catching his face, outlined his jaw, and turned him into an image of the guy in the bookstore.

"Do you have a picture of your grandfather as a young man?" I asked.

"Why?"

"I'm curious to know what he looked like."

He pointed to a wedding picture hanging in the hallway. The face of the stern young man, standing beside his bride's chair, was the same as the man in the bookstore.

How was I going to prove my awakening suspicions about the doctor?

And then I proceeded with a plan that would ruin my sister's life, or maybe save it. To carry it out, I would need DNA from two or more of the children recorded in the red file.

Jim would give me a DNA sample to prove he wasn't his father's son, but he might give me one if I said it was for genealogy, and came in a box marked National Geographic and I paid. So that's what I did. The private detective helped me find a lab that would do the testing without permission. I went back to Sabato and paid him for a sample. I tested myself, and Jan, just in case.

* * *

Two months later I sat in Jenkinson's office waiting for the results.

"I don't usually care what people do with the information I find for them," he said. "But I'm curious. The old guy is dead. You can't charge him with anything. What are you going to do?"

"Jim and Jan need to know. They're talking about a baby."

"I see," he said and handed over the results.

It took me a year to hunt them all down after I convinced the grandson to let me have the files. One of the mothers told me of the "therapy" in the doctor's office that left her with a baby at fifteen. All gave their babies up for adoptions arranged by their doctor, all but the two married mothers.

I had to tell Jan, and then Jim.

"You mean all this time...my brother." She spent the next half hour in the bathroom, vomiting.

Jim walked out without her. They divorced a week ago.

THE WEST COUNTRY

The West Country first appeared in Confabulation 3, an anthology published by Wynterblue Publishing, 2010.

7

THE WEST COUNTRY

*E*ve sat on the edge of the high bed looking around the bedroom. Violet, she thought. Why do the English like this colour? She had stayed in three separate hotels, and all had violet bedrooms. This one was lovely though, a mixture of Art Nouveau and Arts and Craft. But dressing for dinner? Damn, she thought. How was she going to manage that? The brochure hadn't mentioned the need for formal clothes.

She dressed in a green denim skirt, paired with a pale cream silk shirt buttoned, almost, over a lace camisole. Gold hoop earrings, a jade necklace and her black boots finished the outfit. She needed to buy more clothes, if she were going to stay here for a month.

She chose Brake House for its location on Exmoor, in the West Country, its tiny village, Brake Minor, and its Edwardian architecture, her favourite of all English styles. Even the name of the house, Brake, the word in the West Somerset dialect for a piece of land covered with high furze or gorse, was a favourable omen for her work.

What was unexpected was the Edwardian host, Maxwell Liscombe, the fourth in his line to inhabit the house, and keeper of all traditions thereof. He was standing beside the fireplace when she walked into the parlour. Davis, the concierge, now butler as it was after six, announced her. Max turned and placed his glass on the mantle, before walking across the room to shake her hand.

"Welcome to Brake House, Ms Canmore."

"Thank you."

"Davis tells me you are studying the local speech."

"Yes, I'm doing my PhD thesis on the syntax of the West Country dialect."

"Dialects, I suppose you mean," he said. "We can tell hereabout where a man comes from within a mile or two."

"Still? Even with television and the schools?"

"We still have grannies, and they still mind the bairns," he said, as he smiled down at her.

"My grant will only allow me a month."

"What a shame."

A young woman crept into the room while they were talking, and poured a drink at a table in the corner.

"Jennie, come meet our newest guest."

Jennie was perhaps twenty, almost as tall as her father, sharing his dark eyes and hair. Her cheekbones were higher, her skin paler, and her eyes sadder. She came over to shake her hand and offer her a drink.

Davis reappeared, this time with a young man who limped into the room with the help of a hospital-issue cane.

"Liam O'Connor, our resident patient," Jennie said.

"Shall we go in," our host said when Davis opened the doors to the dining room.

A table meant for twenty stood in the centre of the square room. Another fireplace, this one with ornate Art Nouveau tiles surrounding the firebox, sat empty opposite the doors. The table was set only at one end.

"Liam, Eve is also a writer. She is here working on a thesis."

"What do you write?" Eve asked.

"I'm writing a book about the prospects for peace in the Middle East."

"Dismal," Jennie said.

After dinner, Max toured Eve around the house: two sitting rooms, a library, the dining room, eight bedrooms and five bathrooms. They sat over cognac in the library, talking about her work.

"What a lovely place to work in," she said. "There must be three thousand books on these shelves. Were they collected over the years?"

"Most of them were my grandfather's. Like you, he was a scholar. Liam works here. Once he gets downstairs in the morning, he'd rather stay down."

"What happened to him?"

"A car accident six months ago. He damn near died."

"Then he's made a remarkable recovery."

"Yes, he has. I'm very pleased you've come," he said. "Jennie's mother died last year, Another person in the house, a woman, may help her mood."

The light from the fire played over his face and reflected in his eyes. It was his mood she was interested in, but she had a job to do, so no complications.

* * *

Over the next days, Eve developed her routine, working in a fragile bubble of happiness: mornings in her room, writing; a drive with Max and lunch in one of the charming villages or towns around Somerset; dinner with the others. By the end of the first week, Max was in love with her, and the violet bedroom unoccupied for much of the night.

Eve eased out of Max's bed and across to the door.

"You could stay," he whispered.

"No, I can't."

She turned the knob and gently closed the door, tiptoed down the hall and into her room. Jennie stood at the window.

"What are you doing here?"

"What are you doing to my father?"

"What do you think, Jennie? You're not a child. It's been a year since your mother died. Your father needs a woman."

"If you try to take him away from me, I'll kill you." The words were passionate, but the tone flat, apathetic almost. She stood with her arms at her side, her hands open.

"Jennie, have you had any help, any counselling, or talked to a doctor since your mother died."

"I don't need a doctor; I'm not crazy," Jennie said as she brushed past her and out the door.

Somewhere another door closed. Liam was in bed, too. A safe time to visit the library.

If Liam worked at this desk, she thought, he was very tidy: nothing left on top; the computer closed and locked as was one of the drawers. She hadn't brought her tools.

She visited the kitchen for a glass of milk, to explain her visit downstairs. She hesitated at the door of her room, almost expecting a return visit from Jennie, but it was empty of all but moonlight.

The next morning, Liam was waiting for her in the hall outside the breakfast room.

"What have you been doing to Jennie?"

He grabbed her arm and twisted her around to face him.

"Nothing." She fought off the urge to hurl him to the floor.

"I won't let you hurt her. I think you should leave."

"When my work is done. I have a thesis to finish, on a timetable. I don't have time for adolescent angst."

"Her mother died—"

"Yes, and so has mine, but work goes on. Let me go, Liam, before I start shouting."

When Max arrived, the others behaved as though it was just another morning. Max offered mimosas for breakfast. The bubbles rose in her glass. When they reached the top, she returned his silent toast. Max asked Liam about his work.

"It's going fairly well now."

"Do you have everything you need? I'm going up to London today."

"Thanks. Everything I need is here."

That was good news and bad, she thought. Liam sounded as though he was almost finished, but it meant that he must still have the documents here.

Jennie was asking Liam to go to the village of Brake Major with her.

"Do you mind spending the day here alone?" Max said.

"Hardly alone, Max. There are Davis and the cook, the chambermaids, and the groundskeeper. I want to talk to the cook if that's okay. I understand she's Somerset born and bred."

"Yes, she is. Ask Davis when. He sets the work schedule."

Davis might be a problem, she thought. Perhaps if she told him she wanted to work in the library in Liam's absence, he wouldn't interrupt. Max held to the Edwardian idea that servants shouldn't knock so that she would get no warning.

The others left, and she carried her laptop into the library. The tall windows of the bow front gave a view down the allée of Linden trees to the gate. A sports car followed the others down the drive. Good, she thought, Davis had gone too.

She didn't need to touch Liam's computer. What she was after was old and fragile and priceless. The drawer opened easily enough. The folder, labelled with the call number from the archive, lay under the first printed draft of his book. She turned to the sound of car tires on the gravel drive. Liam and Jennie returning early. She was sitting at her computer, working when Liam burst through the door.

"What are you doing in here?"

"Working. I thought you were gone for the day."

"You've upset her so much; nothing makes her happy. Get out of here. I want to finish my work. I'm leaving tomorrow, thanks to you."

She closed her computer and stalked from the room.

* * *

Another night, and another departure from Max's bed. There was no time left. The clock on the landing chimed three as she passed. The house was silent. No Jennie waiting for her with her sad eyes and empty threats. At least she hoped they were empty. Her father was going to be hurt. No way to prevent that.

She opened the library door. The drapes were drawn, shutting out the moonlight. The light from her flashlight picked out the desk. She inserted the first delicate tool into the keyhole.

"Something I can get for you from the desk?" Max said as light flooded the room. Eve stood to face Max and Jennie and Liam.

"Yes," she said. "You can return the documents Liam stole from the State Archive of Israel, six months ago."

"Liam's not a thief," Jennie said shaking off her father's warning arm.

"Look for yourself."

She focussed on Max, who took a key from his pocket and opened the drawer. He lifted the manuscript and the file and placed them on the desk. He read aloud the words, *State Archive of Israel*, and turned to Liam.

"Are these stolen, Liam."

"Of course not. They allowed me to borrow them. I need them to reveal the roots of the conflict, and who is responsible."

"Stolen," she said, pointing her small pistol at them. "And now I'm returning them."

"You don't need the gun, Eve," Max said.

"I think I do, but I don't want to shoot anyone. Place the files in that bag."

"Why are you doing this to Liam?" Jennie said, sobbing into the sleeve of her sweater.

"Why have you done this to me?" Max said.

"It's my job. I am Mossad."

CLARICE

Clarice first appeared in The Gumshoe Review, January 2010.

8

CLARICE

*H*er blood no longer dripped from the blonde oak table onto the worn green carpet. We watched it change from a liquid pool of scarlet to a sticky, muddy brown while police searched the dining area, tiny, powerful flashlights in gloved hands, ready to pick out the slightest piece of evidence that might contradict the story we told them. A young woman stood nearby, barely old enough, I thought, to go to police college, much less guard a group of hardened criminals such as ourselves.

They carried Clarice away an hour ago, but still we sat, determined to say what needed to be said: Monica, tall, too thin to sit comfortably on the hard chair she chose; Andrea, her opposite in most ways, especially in her inability to restrain herself, even now, from loading a plate with food from the buffet; Denise, practical, hardened Denise, sobbing quietly but fervently in the corner by the window; and me, Althea, originator of our writing group. Clarice had booked the room and called us to come on this day and time. I tried to remember if I had somehow betrayed her.

"How did he find us?" Denise choked out the words.

"Who knows? She probably took a call from him," Monica said.

"How can you say that? She was terrified of him." Andrea, opposing Monica as usual.

"Did any of you tell anyone we were meeting today?" A chorus of angry no's answered.

The policewoman patiently recorded the conversation as her colleagues examined the gun which they found by Clarice's body, and which, we knew, was covered with her husband's prints.

We saw him in the lobby, we told the police, while we were on our way up. Perhaps he had an alibi, a friend or someone who owed him a favor. Clarice would have known.

Clarice, sad, determined, trapped in that unholy marriage to a man who couldn't distinguish his wife from some other possession, his Porsche, say, or his collection of hunting rifles. But he let her spend one evening a week with us. Clarice wrote stories for children; she told him all of us did.

But Clarice wrote other stories and left them with us. Angry, hurt, revenge-filled fantasies of what she wanted to do to controlling, abusive men lay in the depths of my computer, locked into a file named Someday. The newest disk was on the couch when we entered the room. I loaded it into my computer and wiped the disk clean and copied one of my files onto it. Clarice deserved some privacy.

"What else do you know about the husband?" asked the detective, as he sat down across from us.

"What more do you want to know? He made her life hell, and now he killed her."

Monica was determined to keep the detective focused on Robert, whom she had loathed since she fell in love with Clarice.

"Perhaps you could tell me where I might find him?"

"He's a lawyer with O'Brien and O'Brien. Try their office."

Denise had stopped sobbing and was now ready in her take-charge way to answer the questions for all of us.

"Why do you think he left the gun?"

"Maybe he was startled when we called?"

"When did you call?"

"We called from the cab, and then went to get some paper at the shop. Clarice said she had forgotten paper."

Now Monica cried as she had to say Clarice's name.

"Where is it?"

"Where is what?"

"The paper."

The paper was in my briefcase, in a bag from the news-stand in the lobby. I hauled it out for him to see.

"I think you ladies can go now. We have your statements and your addresses. We will have to speak to you later."

Did he believe us, I wondered, as I gathered my belongings, including my computer with its secret, and pulled small gloves onto my hands.

At the lobby door, we hesitated, looking out onto the rainy Sunday morning.

"Let's walk down by the river," I suggested.

As we walked along the wide sidewalk towards the Calgary tower, a coven of tiny warlocks and witches overtook us, all intent on one destination - the local McNally Robinson Bookstore. The shop itself was in darkness, a taller black-robed figure opening the door for each of the little initiates.

"What is going on?" Monica said as she avoided yet another rushing group.

"I think the latest Harry Potter is being released this morning," Denise told her.

"All those sales," Andrea murmured.

"What if the police follow us?" Monica asked me. "How will we get rid of them?"

"Let's turn down here."

I took a route that led to the Bow River. The street was empty except for one homeless person, hunched in a doorway, and another trudging aimlessly along, clutching her bag of belongings.

Our footsteps echoed in the strange silence, peculiar for a big city, which bemused me when I moved here from Toronto, where downtown is never, ever quiet. At least we would hear if anyone was following us.

At the river's edge, we stood in the cold mist and watched the brown water flow slowly under the bridge. I pulled off the gloves and turned them over in my hands as we spoke a goodbye to Clarice. They fluttered away in the wind, down to the river and disappeared. They hadn't fit me anyway.

"Do you think we can go through with this," Andrea asked.

"He tortured her. He's responsible for her death," Monica pleaded.

"But we..." Andrea tried to reply, but her words were lost in tears.

"Andrea's right," Denise said. "We can't do this, even though she wanted us to."

"Let's go back."

Silently we walked towards the hotel. As we turned the corner at the bookstore, we saw the detective standing, one hand holding the coffee he had been drinking as he waited for us to come back. We put our arms around each other as we came up to him.

THE ACCOUNTING

A simple trip to a Bay Street, Toronto investment office reveals financial chicanery and sudden death.

9

THE ACCOUNTING

*a*t 11:30 a.m. on a Thursday morning, the racket I created with my too-loose sandals echoed through the empty lobby of a Toronto temple of capitalism. Half an hour later and the marble halls would be teeming with life as offices emptied of assistants and brokers and CEOs, all seeking food or a smoke.

I'd arranged to meet Robert Todd, the honorary uncle, who had, for years, sent me checks from the trust set up for me by my grandfather.

The trust was substantial, so were the fees, and when the elevator doors opened it was clear where much of the money went. It wasn't the rosewood paneling or the spring flowers on the reception or the oriental carpets underfoot. No, what impressed me was the painting behind her, a scintillating Jack Bush.

"I'm Forrest Macklin for Mr Todd", I said.

The receptionist took me to a sitting room to wait for Uncle Robert.

But Uncle Robert wouldn't keep our appointment. Moments after she left, she returned, screaming along the hall for help and someone to call 911. I followed the sounds and then the crowd to a corner office.

His body slumped over the teak desk, dripping blood from the massive wound in his skull onto the beige carpet below.

"Can't we do something?"

The young receptionist clutched at me and wiped her tears on my arm.

"Come on, Sally. We'll wait out here," said one of the others, a young man in a grey suit and paisley tie. He pried her fingers from my sweater and supported her into the next room.

I didn't care what he did with her. Robert was dead and with his death went my contact with the firm. The computer screen read Macklin Holdings—oil and gold and uranium—the only money I had in the world.

I leaned forward towards the computer, but another man blurted out, "You can't be in there. You'll contaminate the scene."

Everyone's a CSI now, I thought and backed out of the room.

Police arrived, filling up the office with large men who herded us all into a boardroom to wait. And wait. And wait.

A rosewood table, surrounded by high-backed leather chairs, dominated the long room. They muttered their names at me and then forgot me.

Sally sobbed at one side. Beside her, Baker—he of the paisley tie —held her hand. Singh, the CSI wannabe, prowled the room, stopping every two minutes to stare out at the outer office until the policeman who watched us shut the door. Two other women— Angie, a tall red-head, chewing all the polish off her perfect nails, and Louise, an older, comfortable-looking woman wearing a long sweater and clutching a bag with knitting needles poking out the top—sat on the other side. The last man, Ned Anson, took a chair beside me. Too close. Unless they found a note or a gun, one of these people killed Robert.

"Where's everybody else?" I said. Surely the place had more than these six.

"Early lunch," Sally said.

"Did anyone else visit Robert this morning?"

"No."

"How about other people in and out? How many in the last hour?"

"Why are you asking about the last hour?" Singh asked.

"The blood was still dripping so he must have been killed only a little while before we found him."

Angie stopped biting her nails.

"You think someone killed him."

"I didn't see any weapon," I told her, "and I don't think he died from a nosebleed. Why didn't any of you hear anything?"

"Coffee, we were at coffee."

"All of you?"

"In and out," Sally said. "We were all in and out of the coffee room on the other side of the office."

"Why are you here?" Anson said. "You don't usually come here."

"Robert asked me to come. Now I wonder if he found something wrong in my accounts. I wanted to check the most recent ones before the police came, but this guy—what's your name? Singh? — wouldn't let me. Who worked on my accounts? Who had access to them? You, Singh?"

"No. I resent the implication that I'm a thief. Robert may have been killed for some other reason. He handled the trust accounts all by himself, all the time."

"Is that true?"

The rest of them nodded heads or murmured yes.

"No cross-checking, no auditing?"

"Of course the auditors came, once a year," Louise said. "I'm sure you are mistaken about Robert doing something criminal."

"Why are you defending him, the way he treated you?" Angie, the redhead said.

"How was he treating her?" I asked.

"That is no business of yours," Louise said, again in that quiet voice. "You shouldn't be talking about other people's private lives, Angie, especially in front of the police."

Seven heads swiveled to the constable standing at the door, but the urge to talk won over discretion.

"He was tossing her out, after all these years as his assistant and more," Angie answered.

"I suppose you think you'll be the chief assistant around here, now Mr Anson will be senior, just because you're sleeping with him," Louise said.

"She's sleeping with him? What is she talking about, Ned?" Sally's little fists beat on the mahogany table.

"Don't be so naïve, Sally. Ned sleeps with all the new girls," Louise said. Her forehead, smooth from a too-tight facelift or Botox, couldn't keep up with emotions that turned a kind, motherly woman into a harridan. Ned kept his head down and said nothing.

"What have your relations with each other got to do with Robert's death?" Baker said from the end of the table, where he again held Sally's hand.

"Yes, I'm more concerned about my accounts, and what has happened to them. Doesn't anybody know anything about them? Louise?"

"Your accounts are fine, dear." Louise, the mother, had resurfaced. "Robert brought them up to date just this morning."

"If you hadn't taken out a hundred thousand last month, you wouldn't need to worry," Anson whispered into my ear, so close I smelled his musky after-shave and smoky breath.

"I didn't take any money out of the account last month, and I thought you said Robert handled my account all by himself. How do you know?"

How much more was missing? Worse, how much was left?

"I've been doing a little snooping. I have a responsibility to the firm."

"Is my money all there now? Louise, you must know?"

"I told you he put it back this morning. You have nothing to worry about. Do stop fussing about your damn money. Robert is dead." Louise's tortured face crumpled as she started to cry.

Black rivulets stained her face, and the dyed hair and the Botox couldn't conceal her fifty years. She pulled knitting and magazines and makeup out of her bag. A hairbrush, matted with blonde hair, grey at the roots, skittered across the table. She clutched a pill bottle. Her shaking hands couldn't cope with the childproof cap, and it skated after the hairbrush. Ativan, I noticed, when I took off the top and handed the bottle back to her. Louise swallowed two tiny tablets.

"What was he doing in the first place? Why did he take such huge sums out of my account? Who was he spending it on—you?"

"Do I look like some man has been spending vast sums on me? Don't be ridiculous. I am sure he was trying to make you some more money. You go through a lot."

"I haven't spent a cent in six months. What are you talking about? How much is left, Louise?"

"It's all there. Robert recovered enough from other accounts to fill yours. There are going to be some unhappy people when the auditors come."

"Whose accounts did he pilfer?"

"All of them."

Astonishing how matter-of-fact she sounded, as though dozens of lives weren't destroyed, hopes and dreams deferred and retirements shattered because Robert was a thief. Or was he? Perhaps she stole the money and Robert were covering for her.

Louise went on. "If you want to know whom he spent it on, look around. I'm not the one with the designer suits and shoes and watches and jewelry. Look at Miss Angie."

Ned Anson's head came up off his arms at that. Angie stopped trying to repair the mess she had made of her hands and glared at Louise and babbled at Anson.

"She's just vicious and jealous, Ned. Pay no attention to her."

"I wondered how you could afford all the new clothes on the

money I gave you," he said. "What happened? Did he threaten to turn off the supply?"

Sally shrieked again from the end of the table. "You gave her money? And pizza and beer for me?"

"Sweetie, try to get the concept, you were a snack. Angie was the main course," Louise said to the sobbing girl.

What a nice bunch, I thought, all with a good reason to want Robert dead. Baker and Singh left their seats and prowled the room, ending up side-by-side at the window furthest from the table. They whispered together, likely about how this would affect their nascent careers while they listened to their co-workers meltdown.

The shrieking at the table stopped. We froze like characters in some Victorian tableau.

Louise was standing. A gun gripped in her shaking hands, wavered between Sally and Angie. The policeman pulled his weapon and shouted at Louise to "put it down".

I don't think she heard him. She was screaming at the girls, accusing them of killing Robert, threatening to shoot them both.

"Put it down, Louise," Anson said, in a quivering parody of the boss's voice.

"You." She turned the pistol towards him. "You killed him too."

Another policeman entered the room, shouting at her to give up her weapon. Her mouth opened, but no sound came. A line of white formed on her lips and dribbled onto her chin. More police pounded in, waving at us to get down, but I stayed on my feet too long and saw too much. Poor Angie. Louise's blood and brains splattered her hair and dripped like tears down her face.

When the detectives emptied Louise's bag, they found Robert's suicide note. He didn't mention her name.

The End

RAIN

Going to the cottage was never more dangerous. **Rain** first
appeared in <u>Canadian Tales of the Mysterious</u>, Red Tuque Books,
Volume 5, 2015

RAIN

I hated rain. Traffic crawled bumper to bumper that Friday afternoon going north to Muskoka like it always did, every Friday. Like I knew it always did, every Friday. So why was I driving through rain so heavy the only thing ahead was a faint pink glow from the taillights of an SUV?

An irate call from my cousin Louise interrupted a lovely free afternoon, which I planned to spend reading and watching the weather move down the lake from the window of my penthouse. Furious, Louise was, all because of a little research into the family I included in a note to her mother. Must have upset Aunt Natalie to find out the story her grandmother told her about our descent from the English peerage was so much, well, pure invention, let's say. I was on my way to explain. Not that Natalie was going to be happy with the evidence I was bringing.

Steam rose from the pavement to meet the wall of water. The traffic guy on the radio said there was a serious accident on Highway 11 at a spot about two miles behind me. At least it was behind me. A signboard loomed through the haze, indicating an off-ramp. I pulled back with a heart-stopping swerve as a small blue car sounded its tiny horn as it passed me on the right on its way down the ramp. I followed him off.

Half a dozen cars pulled onto the township road that ran east to west and parked, waiting for the rain to ease up. I turned west and crossed over highway 11, towards Lake Muskoka, and Port Sandfield. I'd been along this road before, on the way to visit Aunt Natalie, Uncle Gordon and Louise. They didn't ask me to the cottage, probably because of a tendency to argue a bit too much when I drink. One reason I gave up first liquor and then wine a few years ago.

A gas station and a diner sat on the north side of the township road. The lights above the pumps blinked through the rain and I turned into the station. A small culvert carried a steady stream of muddy water from one side of the dirt lane to the other. The downpour had eroded the sides, and my back wheel slipped into a deep rut as I cut the corner a little too short. The car slipped backwards, and the undercarriage caught on the culvert. In seconds I was truly stuck.

The steep angle of the car meant that before I reached my raincoat and laptop in the backseat, I had to climb out. Out and ankle deep in the mud. I pulled my feet out, lost my balance and landed face down in the muck, with rain pounding on my back, plastering my light shirt against my skin and turning my jeans into heavy weights. God, I hated rain.

I staggered across the parking lot, carrying my overnight/laptop bag, the raincoat, my shoes and my muddy purse, and stumbled through the screen door of the diner. A tall, pale, red-haired girl stood behind the counter.

"Bathroom?" I said, dumping my shoes at the door.

She pointed to the left, past the counter. As I sloshed past the only table to the left, I flung my dripping coat onto a chair.

I washed off the mud in the sink, and changed into a clean pair of jeans and another t-shirt. I carried a towel in my bag, one of those small ones that are supposed to dry your hair quickly when you're traveling. When I finished getting water and grime out of my hair, I turned my attention to my face. An attractive blob of clay clung to my nose, and my sandy hair was drying into a curly sheep-dog look. No amount of make-up is going to help this, I thought. I scrubbed at my face, gave up and dragged my bag out and sat down at the nearest table.

"Coffee," the waitress said.

"Yes, please." I took my wallet out of my purse and rooted for my CAA card.

I looked up at the jangle of a teaspoon. The hand holding the cup shook so badly the coffee spilled over into the saucer. Tears threatened to course down over cheeks that were too pale, even for a redhead.

"What—" A minute shake of her head stopped me.

"Thank you," I said loudly. "What's wrong?" I whispered.

"They shot Matt, my husband. I think he's dying."

I dialled my cell.

"You, put down the phone," the man nearest me bellowed as he swung out of his seat. I did, but I connected to 911. I left it connected as I said, "Are you going to shoot both of us. I'm calling CAA to come for my car. What do you call this place?" I asked the woman in the loudest voice I dared use.

"Hennessy's," she said.

"Hennessy's," I said again as loudly as I dared.

"Give me that phone." He grabbed the phone off the table and demanded, "Who is this?"

The person at emergency number must have disconnected or knew enough to be quiet because he threw it back on the table in disgust. I speed-dialed my aunt before he took it back from me.

Again I left it connected.

"I'll shoot you if you don't leave the fucking phone where it lays."

He meant it, too. He pulled an ugly little gun out of his pocket and waved it in my face. Aunt Natalie was saying hello but fell silent. I hoped either the emergency service operator or Natalie called the police. I sure wasn't going to have another chance because my phone broke into several pieces when it hit the wall.

"She says her husband is hurt. I'm a doctor. Maybe I can help him."

"Forget it."

For the first time, I noticed the others in the room. Two other men sat at a table near the door, both still wearing their raincoats. The one who grabbed my phone dropped his gun back into his pocket and sat down again. The waitress sank into the chair opposite me and put her head down on her arms. Her shoulders heaved, but no sound came.

"Hey, you, more coffee over here."

"I'll get some," I said and walked over to the pot.

The three men fell silent as I refilled their cups.

"Did you just come off 11?" one said.

"Yes."

"What's the traffic?"

"Awful. An accident happened two miles behind me, but it was moving a bit where I was. No visibility, so I got off."

"Turn the TV to a news channel."

They were waiting for someone else or for the traffic to clear up. Why did they shoot the husband?

The news was the usual out of Toronto on the all-headline station-lots of crime with an occasional human-interest story tucked in to relieve the gloom. The one on at the moment was a reporter's dream, human interest and crime. Some guy who came up from the Maritimes prepared to kill a lot of people, met a friendly dog in a park, decided that if the dogs were friendly, the people must be good and turned himself in. Half a dozen weapons, ammunition and grenades in his car, enough to kill the hundreds he had planned. A Brinks truck had been robbed, the driver shot, but not killed... and so it went, in spite of a falling crime rate, according to the statisticians.

"The guy's not dead," the man with the gun said.

"Shut up," the man at the next table said. The boss, I supposed.

So that was it. They robbed the truck and thought they killed the driver or the guard. Desperate men. The man in the back room lay dying. Maybe I could talk them into letting me see him since the other one survived.

"I'm a doctor; maybe I can help the guy in the back room.. Don't want to go down for murder, do you?"

I hoped I sounded braver than I felt. My tongue was sticking to the roof of my mouth and I had to force the words out past the big lump in my throat. Globus hystericus was the medical term, but only when the danger wasn't real. This situation didn't qualify.

"Maybe you better let her, Mike. I didn't want to shoot him anyway. Why did you make me do that?"

"Shut up. Ok, go look at him, but the whiner here goes with you."

I edged away, past the counter and into the kitchen. A young man propped against the wall held a wadded-up tea towel against the wound in his leg. Blood stained his jeans and pooled into a gel the color of a good burgundy where it hit the floor. No pumping, so maybe not an artery.

"I need my bag," I said to the guard. "It's in my car."

"You brought bags in with you."

"My medical bag's in the trunk. The keys are in my purse."

When he went to the door to ask, I had a look at the wound. The bullet missed the artery but smashed the bone, I thought, judging from the angle the lower half of the leg made with the upper. He'd lost a lot of blood into the leg and onto the floor.

"I'll give you something for pain when he brings my bag," I said. He didn't answer, just stared at me for those pain-filled eyes, barely conscious. I found a pair of scissors in the kitchen and cut off the leg of his jeans.

"My wife?" he breathed more than said the words.

"She's okay." He closed his eyes again. I tucked the scissors under the pile of cut-off denim.

The man guarding us walked back from the door with my bag as I cleaned the wound with peroxide that I found in the cabinet over the refrigerator. Must have been shot from behind, I thought. The exit wound was in the front. The man gagged in the background when I pulled out a package of needles and attached one to a syringe.

"Fuck," the guard muttered and went down in a dead faint, crashing against the door on the way.

The other two hit the room with their guns out, tripping over their buddy's body as they came through the door. They stopped, confused at seeing me six feet away and on my knees beside Matt.

"What did you do to him?"

"Nothing. I think he has a problem with needles."

"Help him," he, the boss, said.

"He doesn't need any help. He fainted. He'll come out of it in a minute." I didn't look up from dressing the wound.

"Louie, get Drake out of here," the one I decided was the boss, ordered.

Matt's breathing was smoother. I eased him away from the wall and covered him with a couple of coats from hooks by the door. Outside had looked so inviting, I'd almost taken off through the door. Maybe Matt tried, and that was why he was lying on the kitchen floor.

"You. Back out here."

"I should stay with him."

"Out."

An OPP cruiser stood at the tanks. The steady drum of the rain on the tin roof of the diner filled the silence. The policeman hung up the hose and walked towards the door.

"What are we going to do?" That was the one called Drake, recovered from his faint, sitting pale and sweating near the window.

"Shut up. You two," the boss said to the waitress and me, "one word and he's gone."

He was so young, I thought, as I looked at the open, fresh-faced face of the OPP.

"Hi, Tanya," the cop said. He looked around at each of us the way cops do and sat on one of the red stools at the end of the counter. "Where's Matt?"

"He's not feeling good. He stayed home today."

"That's a first."

He swivelled on his stool and asked, "Which of you owns the Toyota blocking the road out there?"

"That would be mine. I slipped off the shoulder in the heavy rain."

"Hung up pretty good."

"I called the CAA."

"You and a hundred others. You'll have a wait."

Tanya put a container of take-out coffee beside his mug.

"Thanks," he said, and strode out of the diner, taking hope with him.

The whiner, Drake, started at Mike, the boss again. "What are we going to do? I don't think she's coming. Why did you let her take the dough?"

"Because they're looking for men. It was safer with her. Now shut up."

"Stop telling me to shut up. I got as much right to the money as you have, and she's your girl. Maybe you told her to take off, and you would meet up with her later. None of it went down the way you said. I want my share and to get out of here."

"Come on, man. I didn't order up the weather. She'll be here."

"Maybe she was in the pile-up on the highway," I said.

"You can keep your mouth shut, too."

"Maybe she's right. Turn the TV on again," Drake said, turning to me.

I turned on the news channel again. Now they showed a

surveillance video from outside the bank. The men sat and watched their images play out a scene lifted from a made-for-TV movie. It went wrong when Mike's mask slipped, and one of the guards saw his face. The video captured the shooting and the surprised look on the guard's face as he went down, but no picture of Mike or the other two.

"They don't know who we are."

"Where the hell is she?"

The next shot was of the highway pile-up, but there was so much water on the camera lens and the window of the helicopter, it was impossible to pick out any one vehicle.

"Fuck. Turn the damn thing off."

I thought I would try again. "I need to look at my patient again."

"Yeah, go."

Drake's voice arrested me. "Another car's turning in."

The car stopped next to mine. Oh no, I thought, not them. Louise was driving with Aunt Nicole just visible in the back seat, but I knew she would be talking.

Uncle Gordon got out and looked at the undercarriage of my car. Now he was dressed for rain: yellow slicker, wide-brimmed hat and matching yellow wellies.

Uncle Gordon got back into the car, drove up, and parked in front of the door.

Aunt Nicole came through the door talking. "Do you believe this girl? Calls me from the road and drops the phone right in the middle of the conversation. Makes me think she is in an accident or something. It's taken us hours to find her."

Nicole sent around her brilliant social smile, not noticing the revolver Drake cradled in his big mitt. Five feet tall, she was dressed today in a tight black top, cut-off jean shorts tied up with a multi-coloured scarf, all visible through one of those clear plastic rain-coats, and topped off by her hair, its colour de jour bright maroon. Aunt Nicole would be seventy-five years old in December.

Uncle Gordon was her second husband, an Englishman. He reminded me of those blonde fighter pilots in the WWII movies, the ones who didn't make it back from the dogfights. He never spoke about his past, and he was too young to have been one of them, but still carried an air of mystery and command. His hand tightened on my shoulder.

"Aunt Nicole, we have a situation here—"

"Now, dear, come and sit down and tell me what was so important you had to drive all the way up here on such a terrible day."

Again she sent around her encouraging smile only this time she saw the gun and screamed.

"Shut her up, doc," Mike snarled at me.

But Gordon did the shutting up, putting his hand over Nicole's mouth and whispering into her ear while he moved her to the table where Louise sat, making herself as small and inconspicuous as possible. With a mother like Nicole, she'd a lot of practice at trying to fade into the woodwork. I tried again to get back into the kitchen.

"I need to check Matt again, and I want to take Gordon with me. He's a surgeon," I lied. "He can help me with the wound."

"No."

"What if they catch you? I can say how you let me help him. It would go better for you."

"Let her go. I don't want the guy to die, and I'm the one who'll go down." Drake wasn't whining now. I heard the dangerous change in his tone, and I thought by the surprised look on his face that Mike did too.

"Go."

Drake followed us in. The harsh sound of Matt's breathing filled the room. He was unconscious now, making no response as I called his name and tried to arouse him.

I whispered to Gordon as I pulled out my faithful syringe, "This guy goes out when he sees a needle. I'm going to give him some morphine if I have time."

I filled the syringe with morphine and called to Drake.

"Can you come help us turn him over so Gordon can look at the other side of the wound?"

"Sure." He was so intent on being helpful I was almost sorry when I held up the syringe as he approached. His eyes rolled, and he slumped again. Gordon caught him before he hit the floor, and I pushed the needle into one of the big veins in his arm. Gordon and I went back to Matt, leaving Drake lying in the middle of the floor.

"I hid a pair of scissors, " I said, pointing to the pile of denim. Gordon pocketed the scissors, while I searched in my bag for anything else we could use to protect ourselves. I had a bottle of Ativan, and a few samples of Risperdal M. Ativan was a fast-acting anti-anxiety medication that would put someone right out if they got enough. Risperdal M is an anti-psychotic, but I had no idea how it would work if dissolved in coffee.

Mike and Louie shouted in the next room, and something heavy hit the floor. The door crashed open, and Mike followed it into the room.

"What did you do?"

"Again, nothing. He went out when he saw the needle. I think he hit his head this time, so he may be out for a while."

"Get out here."

"I'll be finished as soon as I give him this antibiotic."

"Wake up Drake."

"I can't. Only time will do that."

He snarled and grabbed my arm as soon as I put down the syringe, dragging me towards the door while waving his gun at Gordon. What was all this all about?

Louie lay on the floor, unconscious. An expanding pool of blood stained the black and white floor tiles.

"Why did you do this?"

"He thought he was leaving. Fix him up."

The three other women sat at the table at the end of the room,

Nicole looking very old as she held Louise's hand. Gordon started towards them, but Mike stopped him.

He pointed his gun at Gordon's face. "You help her."

While we worked on stopping the blood and bandaging Louie's head, Mike paced the diner, stopping to stare out rain-streaked windows towards Highway 11. It was dark for four o'clock on a Friday in August. The heavy rainclouds and the wind made it look like November. I loathed November.

Gordon started to clean up the mess of blood, carrying sodden paper towels back to the trash barrel behind the counter. He spread the bloodstain a little further each time he wiped it, moving towards the window.

Mike roared at me. "Turn on the fuckin' TV."

The newsreader wore the unblinking look they all did now, as she read the big words on the teleprompter, pretending she'd memorized the days' events. A girl died in the crash on highway 11. A large amount of money had been found in the car. Investigations were continuing.

Mike picked up a bowl from a table, heaved it at the TV as he howled in rage. Gordon, moving with astonishing speed for an almost seventy-year-old guy, grabbed Mike from behind and plunged the scissors into the arm holding the gun. His howling changed to a cry of pain, and the gun dropped to the floor, sliding over the black and white tiles towards the table where the others sat. Louise, dear quiet Louise, picked it up and aimed it at the struggling Mike.

"That's enough," she ordered. "It's all over."

And it was. I called 911 again, only to learn that police held a position outside the diner, about to begin hostage negotiations. Aunt Nicole waved a white tea towel out the door. As the diner filled with large men and one small woman in uniform, I took Gordon aside.

"How did you manage to do that? One minute you're on your knees on the floor, and the next you had him in a chokehold. I thought you were going to break his neck."

"I could have, Belle, but I thought better of it."

"What organization were you with?"

"MI6"

Families—you never know.

THE END

SNOWSHOES

Escape to the forest provides no safety in **Snowshoes**.

SNOWSHOES

A narrow beam of light danced among the trees, once casting a giant in relief, and then outlining a feathery silver bush. I twisted deeper into the makeshift cave I'd found between two rocks, grateful that I'd chosen a white parka. The heavy boots he wore broke through the snow's crust at every step, and he swore as he went down. I pictured him lying face down in the snow, his knees at an awkward angle with his feet trapped. I pulled my own feet tighter into my body and gripped my snowshoes in front of me like a mask.

"Belle," he called. "Come on, Belle. You know I won't hurt you. I just need to talk to you."

Oh, sure. For the two years, we were together hurting me was a favourite pastime. When I'd glimpsed him leaving the cabin, he was carrying a rifle and tucking something else into his belt. Why did he follow me up here? He was hardly the wilderness type. Most years he wouldn't have made it north of the city and certainly not to a cabin in the bush, complete with outhouse and melted snow for drinking water.

He was back on his feet again. The sounds of his stumbling progress moved slowly away.

I crept out of my safe little cave and raised my head enough to look. He reached the hard-packed snowmobile trail that led to the cabin. Time for me to go.

My snowshoes left their herringbone pattern, little signposts behind me, as I climbed. Snow was falling, and I hoped my prints would disappear, and he would have no trail to follow.

When I saw him last, Friday at the board meeting, he was using his well-practised charm on the directors to convince them to let him take over the company my family owned. Had owned, now that the arrangements were almost complete. He scowled when mine was the only dissenting vote. I thought then he assumed I would vote his way. Ex-lovers have strange expectations.

The roar of the sled brought me back from the past to my immediate problem. My car waited for me down and to the right, but Mark knew that too. I spent my childhood climbing these hills and I remembered a hunting camp on that side of the mountain, a little to the left and a long way down. Once I got there, I could walk out a camp road.

The distant sounds of a snowmobile became a background for my passage down the hill. Night was coming, and the snow was getting heavier as I got to the little clearing around the camp. I sat, sheltered by a tall pine. Only the wind whistling through the upper branches of the tree disturbed the silence. Had he given up with night coming or had he abandoned the snowmobile for skis?

I slipped from tree to tree around the edge of the clearing. After I circled the cabin, I pushed open the door— no locks here in the country. The cabin was much like ours, with an old black wood stove in the centre, a separate room for a pair of bunks, and a rough table in front of the window. A stack of wood by the stove meant I wouldn't freeze.

I didn't freeze, but I didn't sleep either, between the howling of the wind and the pounding of my heart at every errant creak of the cabin's old boards. Before the sun was up, I was strapping on my snowshoes to walk out. The wind died, and the temperature rose overnight. Water splashed down from the icicles on the overhang and froze again just in front of the door. It would be heavy going through the wet snow. The smoke from the chimney outlined a lazy-s against the pink-streaked morning sky.

An engine roared behind me. Whether Mark's machine or someone else's, I couldn't tell, but then it stopped somewhere, likely at the cabin. The smoke betrayed me. Now I had a new goal, a ski resort that occupied most of this side of the mountain but I didn't remember how far away it was.

The thick bush ended at a clearing punctuated by the gnawed remains of birch and aspen trees. Beaver meadow, we called it when I was a child. I picked my way across, avoiding the spikes that would ruin my snowshoes and end any chance I had of eluding Mark.

Past the wide expanse of the beavers' café, I stopped again to listen. I wondered if I dared to cross the pond formed by the dam built by the energetic little rodents. The ice might hold my weight. It was a long way round to get to a narrow spot on the creek where crossing would be less risky. The crashing of machinery in the bush behind me startled a foraging black squirrel that chattered at me from the top of the dam.

"Right," I answered. "Straight across the dam it is."

I took off my snowshoes and picked my way across the top. Those dam-builders did fine work. It held my weight, and I made it to the other side and started up. The snowmobile's roar came closer, and as I reached the trees, it appeared across the meadow. I hoped he would get hung up on the stumps, but he made it to the shore of the pond. At least he would have to go around the pond, and that would give me a little time.

The engine revved and the machine accelerated straight towards me across the pond. He got about halfway before he went through. He flailed in the water until he reached the ice, threw his arms onto it and tried to pull himself out but it broke into shards, dropping him back into the water. I searched for deadfall or branches to break off, anything to reach out to him, but there was nothing.

"Belle," he screamed. "Belle, help me."

"I'll get help. I can't pull you out myself."

"Don't let me die."

"I'll go for help, Mark. The ski hill is just over the ridge."

The heavy wet snow held me back, but I made it to the top at last. Far below, Mark was moving in the water of the pond. Ahead of me, the top of the chairlift showed through the trees.

The gaily-clad skiers stared at me as I slipped and slid across the hard-packed snow. The attendant started to tell me I couldn't be here.

"A snowmobile went through the ice back there," I interrupted. "The guy can't get out."

I rode with the rescuers back to where I'd left him. When we got to the top of the rise, the black hole remained in the pond, but not Mark. They found him under the ice. They found his rifle on the snowmobile.

I

THE EMPTY ROOM

A journey to the Middle East takes a young woman deep into the truth of her relationship with her husband

THE EMPTY ROOM

I crossed to the window overlooking the garden and threw open the shutters. A trumpet vine, wending past on its way to the sun held a hummingbird in one of its orange blossoms. The iridescent shape darted from one flower to another until it hovered, helicopter-like, inches from my face. The tiny bird stared at me for long seconds before it gave an angry buzz and flew away to the Ginko tree. I turned back to the room, empty except for a hovering estate agent, and mentally measured the floor space.

"What do you think, Mrs Grant?"

The nervous agent interrupted my calculations, and I hissed, sounding exactly like the hummingbird. The poor woman took a step back.

"I'm sorry, Ms Foster. I think the house will suit us. I'll send my husband pictures tonight and get back to you in the morning."

"Several other viewings are booked for today, I believe."

Several other viewings indeed, with the real estate market dead for years now. "No doubt, but I still must call him, and he's in Dubai. Is the fireplace useable?"

"Oh, yes. Wood or coal."

Wood or coal? How easy were they to get?

Two months later, I knelt in the same room, on the Isphahan rug that I brought with me from Canada, the only thing of mine in the house. I put a match to the kindling in the fireplace, even though the fire did little to take the chill of the room away. The deep coral and pale grey accents of the rug echoed in the drapes at the window and the cushions on the blue velvet sofa. I detested that sofa.

Simon rushed down the stairs.

"The cab's here, Adrienne. I have to go. Don't get up, darling," he said and waved a kiss to me.

"Soon you'll be living in Dubai full time."

"I'll be home in ten days." And he was gone. Again. Without me.

"You wouldn't like Dubai," he said. He should know. He'd worked there for three years, all the time they were Internet dating and then meeting for his long holidays in romantic places like Venice and Nice.

Why not? Several of my friends, well, his colleagues' wives, lived out there and wrote to me—emails about the rich life. Mostly they shopped, though, and I didn't much care for that. Perhaps Simon meant that I'd find nothing to do.

Nothing for me to do here either. The house was a mistake—country living, on the edge of a village, walk to the pub and the post office cum store. How enticing it had sounded. Places I never went. Thirty miles to the only decent grocery store and as for the pub, the one time I ventured inside, there'd been nothing but disinterested stares and silence. And then the walk back through the grisly mist that seemed to envelop the village every night. Once was enough.

Two months during which Simon had been away at least six weeks.

The outside door opened. The housekeeper dropped her purse to the floor before she hung up her heavy wool coat.

She, Jackie, bustled about taking the vacuum from its closet under the stairs, putting the kettle on for the tea she needed before she got started for the day and opening the kitchen window to let in the fresh air.

Nothing for me to do. I loathed housework and Simon had insisted on Jackie. "You had help in Canada."

"What work did you do at home?" Jackie asked when they met.

"I'm a doctor."

"You didn't want to work here?"

"Simon felt we would be tied down too much if I couldn't leave as spontaneously as he could."

I hadn't gone anywhere since we arrived.

But I couldn't have gone with him all these times. I needed to settle into the house, arrange the furniture, buy new things. Not that we bought much. His mother's possessions stuffed every room, and he wouldn't part with any.

Settle in. The longer I stayed, the more unsettled I felt.

The post rattled through the door. A brochure escaped the bundle I picked up and sorted, some for the basket, some for Simon's desk. A bright blue sky hung over the towers of a city on the cover of the brochure. Dubai again. A tour, hop on, hop off anytime in 24 hours or 48. I could go, stay with Simon for two days and come home. No bother to him, but I could see the city, and where he lived. A small flat, he said, with room enough for one. Surely room enough for me for two days. I'd surprise him.

Two days later I landed in Dubai in the early afternoon. The immense airport, with more up-scale shopping than I'd seen anywhere but London, palm trees in a park in the middle of the terminal, and kiosks selling phones covered in jewels, confused and disoriented me when I left customs. I wandered, perched in an armchair, and waited for my mind to become used to the chaos: random voices, snippets of conversation, sudden rushes of passengers, gaggles of Indian shoppers in brilliant saris of gold and blues and reds punctuated by anonymous shapes in burqas, or European women, dull in beige and white. Overriding all the scent of flowers I didn't recognize, and the aroma of spices—cumin and garlic and coriander all mingled with French perfume.

I didn't have a plan for getting from the airport to the apartment. Would the drivers speak English? Maybe I should take a shuttle to a hotel, a Hilton or Marriott or something else familiar and reliable, and call Simon to come for me. A tourist information booth promised help in English.

"I need to make a reservation at a hotel, please. Can you do that for me?"

The young woman behind the desk smiled and asked which hotel I preferred. Which hotel? A board showing shuttle service held names of hotels. I chose one I recognized.

"Crowne Plaza, please."

"For one?" Should I say for one? What were the rules here?

"I'm expecting my husband to meet me. Best make it for two."

"He will have to register, Madame."

The hotel room could have been anywhere, but the road outside, the hotel building, the lobby, all reflected glitz and glamour and indulgence. Simon was right. I wouldn't like it here; didn't like it here. I'd wait until after office hours, call his mobile and tell him where I was and then I would go to his flat. The hotel would arrange a car or a taxi for me after I spoke to him.

I took a shower, and washed the travel out of my hair and made up carefully. But Simon didn't answer my call.

"I will wait for you, Madame," said the hotel driver. "If your husband is within, please send him to tell me."

"That is very kind, but you needn't bother."

"Oh, no, Madame. The hotel is very strict."

I walked across the blue-tiled courtyard to the bank of elevators. His number was 2705. I rang the doorbell and waited. How surprised he would be.

The young woman on the other side of the chain, her dark hair pulled back from an oval face, carried a baby, six months old or so, on her hip. "Yes?"

"I'm sorry, I must have the wrong flat. I'm looking for Simon Grant."

"He is away on business. He will be back tomorrow."

"Are you his housekeeper?" Oh, please, let her be the housekeeper.

She laughed, a tinkling, young girl's laugh. "No. No. I am his wife."

"My name is Adrienne. I'm staying at the Crowne Plaza. Please tell him when he gets back."

I held the tears back while in the elevator and in the lobby, surrounded by people—English people they seemed, most of them —and across the courtyard. In the back of the hotel car, I choked on my tears.

"What is wrong, Madame? Are you ill?"

"No, not ill. Take me back to the hotel."

"Was your husband not at home?"

"No. She said she was his wife. His wife and his baby. We've been married three years. Or not married, if he married her first."

"A wife and a baby?"

"Yes. She looked so young."

I shouldn't have said anything. They had strict rules here, about sex and marriage and living together. Tomorrow I would get back on the plane and go back to England and wait for Simon.

A traffic jam. The temperature in the car overwhelmed the air conditioning, and my scalp was sweating and my knees. I hated when my knees did that. When the taxi reached the entrance to the hotel, the driver helped me out.

"I am so sorry, Madame."

"Thank you."

And then I was back in the anonymous hotel room. What should I do? What possible explanation could there be? I stared out her window at the nightscape of the city, all twisted towers in surreal shapes, a city out of a science fiction movie.

A knock at my door.

"Madame. The police are here to speak to you." The police. My chest tightened; something had happened to my breathing. I'd forgotten how to breathe. I gripped the back of a chair as the room swayed. The knock came again.

"One moment."

I steadied and walked to the door.

Two men in uniform stood at the door, the taxi driver behind them. One of the men said something, a question to the driver.

He answered him and stammered at me, "I am so sorry, Madam. It was my duty—"

A harsh word from one of the police cut him off and sent him scurrying away.

"Will you come with us downstairs, please?"

"Yes."

I gathered up my purse and my phone and my passport and walked out with them and down the elevator. What would I do? What if Simon wouldn't help me?

They took me past the reception desk and into an office with French windows opening to the courtyard. The manager waited for them.

They began a three-way conversation between the officer who seemed to be in charge, and me, and the manager stuttering his apologies.

"Where is your husband, Madame?"

"I only know where I expected him to be." I gave them his address and his workplace.

"The driver said a young woman was in his flat. Was that true?"

"Yes."

"Did you expect her to be there?"

"No."

"Did your husband expect you?"

Oh, God, what had I done? Were they going to arrest Simon? The other officer was thumbing through her passport. He handed it to the interrogating officer.

"No. I wanted to surprise him."

"You are Canadian?"

"Yes."

"And your husband?"

"British."

"And you live in England as man and wife?"

"We are man and wife. We married three years ago in Toronto, Canada, in Trinity United Church. My parents—"

"Thank you, Madame. We ask you to return to your room. Do you have a male relative here that you can call?"

"Only my husband. My brother is in Qatar, working at a hospital." David would come. That's what I would do. Call David.

"His contact information?"

I fumbled with my phone, my sweating fingers slipping on the screen until I found my list and David's address.

"Yes, a surgeon. He's helping set up the children's hospital."

"We will call him."

"Thank you. What about my husband?"

"We will speak to Mr Grant."

I took the elevator alone to my room and sent a frantic text message to David. And then I sat and stared at the skyline of the city I would never know.

"Adrienne. The police called. They want me to come for you. What the hell is going on?"

I told him and listened to the silence for long minutes. Waited for the "I told you, so".

"I'm so sorry, Boo. I'll reach you in a couple of hours."

Tears flowed at his childhood name for me. I waited.

Another knock at the door.

"Madame, your brother is here."

I flew to the door, took a deep breath and opened it.

"David. Please come in."

He sat beside me on the couch and took my hand.

"I called the detective back. They've arrested Simon and the young woman. They married here six months ago. He's facing a lot of charges, Adrienne."

"What should I do?"

"What we must do. I'll take you to Qatar or back to Britain, whichever you want. But we are required to leave on the same plane. They don't want you wandering around, talking to the press."

"The press! God, no. I want to go home. Please take me home."

A month later, I put the address on the last box and watched it loaded on the truck. I'd put Simon's mother's things in storage, sold the rest of the furniture, and sent the money and the receipt to him, care of the prison. Six years. How would he stand six years? The lawyer said he would appeal to reduce the sentence. The doorbell rang.

"I've come for the keys, Mrs Grant."

"Doctor Bailie."

"Pardon?"

"My name is Doctor Bailie."

I closed the shutters in the empty room.

JACK'S LUCK

An overheard conversation and a bet on a horse end in tragedy.

Jack's Luck first appeared in Confabulation 3, Wynterblue Publishing, 2010.

JACK'S LUCK

*J*ack's hand stopped on its way to his mouth with his third beer of the morning. The voice behind him had said fifty to one.

"What ya mean, put it on the fifty-to-one shot. What's the name?"

"Jack's Tavern."

"Helluva name for a horse. Never heard o' him. No chance."

"Sure you have. See that's the thing. This horse used to be called Thunder-Ball when he raced out east. He won lotsa races. One o' them sheikhs owns him, and I heard the fix is in."

"Ya, I remember. He's by Thunder-Fruit outa Lion Maid."

"Thunder-Fruit! Helluva name for a stallion." Both men laughed and went on talking, but Jack had stopped listening.

Fifty-to-one, he thought. Maybe it was a sign that his luck was changing. His name was Jack, and here he was in a tavern. If he put together a thousand, he'd pay the sharks and leave Lucy and go to Houston. Start over, without her, and her whining, and her mother, and her damn dog. Well, he'd miss the dog.

Fifty-to-one. His brother, Tony had the money, but said no

more, not ever. Alana, his brother's wife owed him. He hadn't told Tony about their affair. That's what he'd do. He'd see Alana.

He left the tavern, singing his favorite song, the one his dad always sang. All he remembered was "I'll be in Scotland afore ye." And the mournful tune, but Dad sang it when things were looking up. He pulled his change out of his pocket. Two quarters and a transit token. It was enough to take him to Tony's building. The streetcar rumbled behind him, and he ran a little to reach the stop.

He rode to the end of the line and walked a half-mile further to his brother's waterfront building. The security looked him over, but let him go up when Alana said it was okay.

Alana was a little Venus—five feet tall, pocket-sized but curved in all the right places and a red head, his favorite. He could have kept her, except for his brother and all that money, and the collapse. Damn Wall Street. Instead, he had Lucy and her mother.

She had on a purple thing, one of those that tie in front and invites you in. She'd changed for him, he thought.

"Hey, Alana."

"Hey, yourself. Come in."

She gave him a rye and drank one with him and talked about how unhappy she was and how bored with Tony, and all the time her eyes dared him to make a move. When he didn't, she sat up straighter and pulled in the robe or whatever, and asked why he was there.

"We have a chance to make fifty thousand if you can spot me a thousand to put down.

"A thousand. Why would I give you a thousand?"

But he saw by the sudden fear in her lovely eyes that she knew why.

"Because of what we meant to each other."

"I don't have it, not in cash. You know he doesn't let me have much cash."

"What about your jewelry?"

He could see she was thinking. Her share of fifty thousand would take her away from Tony, out of his control.

"Okay. I have that diamond and emerald bracelet with the valuation too. It's worth ten thousand."

"So we can raise a thousand on it."

He waited and drank more rye while she dressed and got the bracelet. They took her car to the pawnbroker and then the track.

He sent Alana to buy the ticket at the crowded wicket. None of the guys who worked for his bookie hung around, but he couldn't take any chances.

They stood at the rail and cheered and yelled and hugged each other when Jack's Tavern came in a length ahead of the field. He sent her for the money. Maybe she won't come back, he thought. Now she has the money, she can just leave, buy back her bracelet and she'll be free of Tony.

But, here she came, a bouncy, happy little doll, patting the purse stuffed with their winnings and stretching up to give him excited kisses.

"Come on," he said. "And watch. We don't want any company."

He drove. She wanted to, but he needed to leave fast. He owed a hundred thousand to Fat Edward, and word would get to him. It always did. But they had the money, fifty one-thousand dollar bills. Jack started whistling his dad's song. Alana turned on the radio.

"Scandal brewing at the racetrack at this hour. The fifty-to-one shot, Jack's Tavern, ran a superb race. No question about it.

Problem is, the stewards have learned that the horse is Thunder-Ball running under a false name and should have been the down-right favorite. Investigators will be contacting all the big winners today."

Alana screamed.

"Jack, what are we going to do? I had to give my name. They'll be calling Tony. Will they arrest me? What am I going to do?"

She was pulling at his sleeve and crying.

"Shuddup and let me think."

Dammit, again. Every time, every time he got a little ahead, he got smacked down. And now he had another whining woman to deal with.

"Jack, we gotta go to the police. We gotta go back."

"No, we're going to Houston."

"They'll stop us at the airport. I want to go home. Take me home."

"No."

She was right about the airport, he thought. They'd drive to Houston. Now she was sobbing and pulling at his arm again. Why couldn't she just shut up?

A flashing light reflected in the rear-view mirror.

"You gave them your name and your license for id, I suppose."

Why hadn't he thought of that? Stupid, stupid. He pounded the steering wheel, swerving out into the lane beside them and back in as Alana screamed again.

The cop was closing in, but the ramp to the interstate was there, and Jack swung into the exit lane. He hit the curve at a hundred, and the barrier at ninety.

The car arced silently through space. No airbags but the seat belt held him back. Alana was quiet beside him as they hit the road below and hung, suspended. The money from Alana's purse escaped and floated past him, the last thing he saw before the darkness.

SUNRISE

Sunrise, a journey into a woman's obsession, first appeared on Women on Writing, 2014 when it won a prize on the site.

14

SUNRISE

a solitary drop stained the windowsill. I stared at it, wishing it away, but there it sat, congealed, changing its color almost as I watched. Of course, there wasn't supposed to be any blood. That's the whole point of poison. Bloodless, quick, quiet, painless: those are the words I associate with it. But it hadn't turned out that way.

I suppose I should have read further in the handbook on poisons I found in the used bookstore. There was likely a section on untoward events or rare possibilities that would account for the blood.

Marnie made a face when she drank her tea. It was supposed to be tasteless too, but perhaps that only applied to the rats.

"I'm going home," she said. "I hope we're okay now."

Sure, okay with you taking the only valuable thing in my whole sorry life. Jake wasn't much of a person, but he was mine, and I loved him, in spite of it all.

Jake called in the morning. He was stuttering. He always stuttered when he lied or when he was scared.

"Can you come over to Marnie's? She's sick."

"Sure."

I wanted to watch, didn't I. Revenge is watching the other person suffer.

I walked the six blocks that separated our apartments, taking my time. If I got there too soon, she might suspect me.

Too slow. I hadn't taken Jake's impatience into account. He could never wait. An ambulance sat at the curb and the body, no, the patient, on the stretcher had Marnie's fair hair. Jake was crying and holding her hand.

"Don't die. Please, don't die," he sobbed into her hair. He saw me and screamed at me, "What took you so long? Why didn't you come?"

I started to answer but the ambulance crew hoisted her into the box, and Jake turned his back on me and scrambled in with her.

I climbed to the second-floor apartment opened the door. This is where she took him to when he left me.

Light flooded the space from the tall windows overlooking the city. Paintings, Jake's paintings covered the walls and stood in stacks against the walls: early works—his cubist phase, he called it— colorful and enigmatic; later ones vaguely Group of Seven, when he painted at the cottage; one appalling portrait of me, rapacious and suspicious. That one hid in a pile near the door and had been the cause of the last big blowup. I know I shouldn't have called him a talentless hack. He didn't paint me again.

His shrouded easel took up one corner. I lifted the cover. He had been painting her. Joy and love for her lay in every brushstroke and filled the painting with light and grace. It was splendid, and I had tried to kill it. He had escaped here, to breathe her air and her freedom, away from me and my suffocating, smothering love. I turned away from her face and let the shroud fall back over her.

The light was fading as I walked back home. Twilight filled the corners of my room with apricot and violet. I sat while the light died and the streetlights blinked on one by one. I sat longer and thought about Jake and his capacity for forgiveness. I had used it up. He wouldn't forgive me this.

The tea was bitter. No wonder she'd made a face although she had been trying so hard to be polite. By sunrise, I felt the poison in my lungs and abdomen and the weakness in my arms. My heart was pounding, pushing what remained of my blood through collapsing arteries. My phone was ringing.

Jake's voice. "They saved her. She's going to be all right."

"That's good; that's good."

"Goodbye, Jake. I love you."

"Bye, Mom."

ABANDONED

A walk in the forest turns deadly, but for whom?

15

ABANDONED

From where I lay, the trees stretched dead or dying to the far-away sky. Grey trunks dropped thin, broken branches to the forest floor.

Down here, the green forest struggled to return, a few scattered whips of understory bushes and soft moss blanketing fallen limbs, glowing in the filtered sunshine. I rolled, fighting pain that coursed up from my shattered ankle. Beneath me crunched the brown leaves, so old and fragile that they powdered under my weight, too old to have any scent but that of the damp earth itself.

He'd left me here, among the fallen. He'd get help, he said.

Maybe. Maybe. But he abandoned me before. Not in the bush, though, not where no one would ever find me, but in the city, that time in Venice when he ran off in a temper, leaving me bereft on a canal somewhere in the desolate north of the city, far from the cafes and music and crowds of tourists. I walked—it seemed for all the day—until I glimpsed one of those orange signs that point the way to Piazza San Marco and followed a twisting course, wandering into dead-ends peopled by black-clad women with suspicious eyes, hanging washing on lines strung high above me.

Here, only grey, fragile branches and above them, the green of what remained alive, came between me and the sun. And what of the creatures that belonged in the forest, the fearful ones, the squirrel and the chipmunks, and the braver, angrier skunks and racoons, and the coyotes, slinking after dark with yellow eyes: when would they come? Day faded into twilight and the blue above to pink and then the navy of late evening, punctuated by a solitary point of light, a star, flickering.

In Venice, I found my way back to the Piazza, the most beautiful in Europe. He laughed when I came upon him, drinking wine in the cafe in front of the hotel.

Where was he now, laughing? I slept, off and on, until the colour returned above me.

Someone shouted, children, crashing through the underbrush. I called, and they stood around me with big, scared eyes, three girls and a boy, stepping-stones from twelve-years-old to five.

"Bring your parents," I said. "My leg is broken."

"Okay."

Something jumped onto the trunk beside me. A black squirrel, its dark eyes staring at me, its tiny paws gripping the tree, carried a chestnut in its mouth as it scrambled up to a nest.

"What was that?"

"Only a squirrel, lady," said the eldest, the boy. "I'll get my dad. The girls can stay here with you."

And they did until rescuers emerged along the path and carried me back to the campsite.

He never came, and when I found him, sitting in our living room, he laughed and said, "I knew you would be all right."

But I wasn't, not then and not now, even though he's dead.

PORTRAIT OF HER FATHER

The soul of the subject, revealed in a painting, takes the artist on a journey to her own past and a disturbing truth.

16

PORTRAIT OF HER FATHER

The wind chime's mellow note floated over the garden, stirred into life by an errant breeze. It ruffled the white hair of the elderly man seated under a tree, his gaze on the top corner of an easel standing a few metres away. He lifted a hand to pat his hair back into place.

"Don't move, Dad," the woman behind the easel pleaded.

"My hair—"

"I'm doing your hands now," she said.

His long fingers curled into white-knuckled fists and relaxed into position again.

Her father died that spring. Anna hung his portrait in the living room, not above the fireplace. He had always said the only appropriate subjects in a painting above a fireplace were horses, dogs or boats. His portrait hung opposite her chair, the one with the best reading lamp and the worst view of the television.

Anna brought her coffee into the living room, her favourite in the house, sunny with tall windows overlooking the garden. She lifted her eyes to her father's portrait.

"What are you doing in here?" her husband asked, when he found her there instead of in her usual morning seat in the kitchen, watching the birds quarrel over the seeds in the feeder.

"Dad's been gone two years today," she said.

"I'm sorry—"

"Don't worry. Do you see anything wrong with the painting?"

"Wrong. What are you seeing?"

"Perhaps I didn't catch his eyes right."

Six months later, Anna stood before her easel, trying to begin again. She'd scraped the painting down three times now, and still, the light on the garden eluded her. She'd chosen a winter scene, snow and tiny red berries clinging to the Euonymous hedge, food for the cedar waxwings that had descended in a flock of ten or more. She'd chosen one, a male with a jaunty crest, that curved his body forward to peck at a berry. But she could catch neither the sheen reflecting off his grey back nor the brilliance of the cluster of ruby berries.

"Stupid girl," she heard her father's voice. "Do it again." How many times had he said that?

"It's beautiful, Anna. Leave it alone," her husband said. "It's time to start another. You've been working on the bird for most of this year."

"Something must be wrong. Like the portrait. Like everything I've ever painted."

"Anna, the gallery called. They want several more canvases, the ones you promised."

"I can't. They're not good enough."

"Yes, they are. Come; look at the portrait. You'll see how terrific it is."

"I don't know, Peter. It bothers me. Something about the eyes."

～

Anna's one-artist show opened to rave reviews, and better, many little red circles indicating sales. She, Peter and the gallery owner stood in the living room, raising glasses of champagne, in a toast to the show and each other. Her father's eyes were on her, from his perch across from her chair. The gallery owner, Desmond, followed her eyes.

"Who is he?"

"My father."

"You painted this?"

"Yes."

"Not your usual approach."

Peter interrupted with a question about taking the show to another city. Not her usual approach, she thought. What had he meant?

～

Anna supervised the installation of her show in the Art Gallery of Ontario. Hours later, she and Peter sat in the living room, sipping wine and talking over the evening.

"You decided against putting your dad's portrait in the show. I thought you wanted to begin with it?" he said.

"Do you remember what Desmond said after the first show, that it wasn't my usual approach?"

"Your usual approach. I thought the point was that you're experimental, edgy. No usual approach."

"It's the eyes."

"What?"

"Look at him."

"What do you see?"

"Malevolence."

"You're serious."

"Yes."

∾

"Anna, can we move your dad's picture somewhere else. It's starting to bother me since you told me you saw evil there."

"Where?"

"What about the attic?"

His papers were stored in the attic. Perhaps his portrait should be as well.

∾

On a rainy Saturday, she climbed up the back stairs to the attic. The light, diffused through the dust accumulation of eighty years, turned the space into a sepia photograph. Trunks, one of them dating back to her grandmother, leather suitcases covered with stickers of the White Star line, hat boxes and anonymous crates filled two-thirds of the space. Closer to the stairs stood her father's file cabinet, an antique of wood and brass. She'd never looked at the contents. He stored his contemporary papers in his office desk or his safety deposit box. These were older, from his early years at the gallery he owned. Mundane for an artist, she thought, nothing but bills and receipts, an occasional note from a satisfied client, reviews for his work from the Globe and Mail and various art journals. She hoped for something more personal, a journal or a diary, something to explain the man she'd known only as a demanding teacher.

Anna sat back, considering her last thought. She only remembered the constant criticism, the names—stupid girl, imbecile, clumsy girl—and the demands for perfection: do it again; scrape it down; the light is wrong; the colour is wrong. Had he loved her as a father?

Anna moved a pile of three hatboxes from the top of a dresser. She would hang the portrait here, where the light from the dormer would fall on it for part of every day. One of the boxes felt heavier than the others. Perhaps an old hat, she thought. Something of her mother's. He'd given away everything that belonged to her mother. When she was old enough to want something of hers—pictures, jewellery, clothes—he said there was nothing, nothing, not even a wedding picture or a photo of her mother holding her when she was a baby.

She opened the box. A pile of old photographs, the edges curling and the colours fading lay on top of a book, a journal, the kind with a small key that young girls used to keep and decorate with flowers and hearts and happy faces. None of that here, though.

The first line. *What have I done? He's not the man I thought he was. Today he called me stupid and a lazy bitch. Yesterday it was can't you do anything right.*

Anna read on, through a year of marriage, her birth, the constant denigration that led to slaps and punches and broken bones and lies. *I told them I fell on the stairs. Why did I say that?*

The last, desperate entry. *I can't go on. My poor baby. How can I leave her behind?*

Her mother died the next day. In a car accident, he told Anna when she grew old enough to ask.

* * *

Anna brought the portrait up the stairs into the attic, looked at it one more time. She hadn't made a mistake with the eyes. She hung the portrait with its face to the wall.

THE DRAWING

A child's journey from abuse to mental health. The Drawing was first published by the Gulf Coast Writers Literary Association in 2013.

THE DRAWING

"*How* long has Olivia been here?" the new doctor asked the head nurse.

"For about six months."

Olivia listened to them. They never asked her how long she had been there, or when she was going home, or why she came. They only asked each other. None of them knew.She sat at the round table in the middle of the sunny room. Others sat on chairs around her, but no one talked to her. Or maybe she didn't talk to them. Or maybe she had forgotten how.

The nurse brought the craft box over to her. "Would you like to do something today?"

The nurse shook her head. "She rarely participates."

Olivia reached into the box and pulled out some paper and colored pencils.

"Are you going to draw a picture?" the doctor asked.

He sounded kind but he might be one of them. She glanced at him from the corner of her eye. If you looked at them too long, they could take your thoughts and hide them.

He sat down in the chair beside her. If she didn't look, he would disappear. They always did. She took a pencil, blue, the colour of the shirt the man wore and started to draw some lines on the paper.

They were talking about her again.

"Her eyelashes have grown back in," the nurse said. "She stopped pulling them about a month ago. When she first came, we had to trim her hair so she couldn't pull it. She was pulling off the skin, infecting her scalp. Now she draws circles with her right great toe, whenever she is standing."

"Perhaps we could talk about that some other time," the doctor said. "Olivia is a little scared."

She looked at him again but only for a second. He was still there. He had stopped the talking. No one had stopped that woman talking before. She took a pink pencil from the box and drew more lines. She was trying to remember how to make the lines mean something important but she had forgotten how. She looked at the doctor to see if he noticed but he was gone.

"How long has Olivia been here?" the new doctor asked the head nurse of the ward.

"A year tomorrow."

"Does her family visit?"

"Only her mother. I haven't met her father. Her mother says it upset Olivia when he used to come."

Olivia listened to them. They still didn't ask her, and she had been here longer than anyone, all her life, perhaps all her life, although she had started to remember the before. The shaking got worse when she remembered and she had to make the circles so it would stop. Or draw.

"She seems to be responding to the art therapy. She always participates in it, and some of her paintings are very lovely."

"Lovely? Nothing to explain what brought her here?"

"Not in the paintings, but some of her drawings are strange."

That wasn't very kind, Olivia thought. She waited until they went away again, and pulled out the papers from her craft box. The blue lines made a man and the pink lines made a girl. She didn't know where they were. She started to shake again and stood up and made circles until the shaking stopped.

"How long have you been here, Olivia?" the new doctor asked.

"She's been here about eighteen months," the nurse said.

"I asked Olivia."

A woman again. The last one had been mean and took her drawings away to show to other people. That's what she said. When they can't take your thoughts they take your drawings.

"I don't know," Olivia said.

The nurse looked funny with her mouth open like that. Olivia laughed. She remembered laughing, long ago, before this place.

"May I see your drawings?"

Oh, no. She will want to take them away like the other one.

"I won't touch them. You hold them and show me."

She showed her the pictures. She had been drawing a long time now. The man in the picture had on a blue shirt and brown pants. He was very tall, much taller than the girl in the pink dress. The girl was lying on the floor. Where were they? She couldn't quite remember. She didn't want to remember. She ran away to her room. She stood in the corner and made circles with her toe for a long time.

"It's been two years since Olivia came here. Has she made any progress?" the new head nurse asked the doctor.

"Yes, she is remember and drawing. I think I understand what happened to her."

Olivia was drawing.

The doctor asked, "May I show your drawing to my friend? I'll give it right back to you."

This doctor didn't take her drawings away. She gave her the picture.

The man with the blue shirt was lying on the girl with the pink dress and she was crying.

"I don't have to make circles anymore."

"Excellent. Who is the man in the picture?"

"The monster."

"The monster?"

"Can you tell me about him?"

Olivia had stopped talking.

"How long have you been here, Olivia?"

"Three years, since I was fourteen."

"Are you ready to leave?"

"Yes, My mother is coming to get me."

"Is your father coming?"

"I don't know."

Olivia and the doctor walked to the front door. Her mother and a man walked up the steps towards her.

"Your father did come," the doctor said.

But Olivia didn't hear him. She screamed and pulled on the doctor's arm.

"The monster, the monster."

The doctor took her back inside and called the police.

THE WEDDING CAKE

The Wedding Cake was first published in Confabulation 4, an anthology published by WynterBlue Publishing, 2011.

18

THE WEDDING CAKE

*B*rittany attached the smallest tip to the pastry bag and scribed the letters onto parchment paper. She always did a trial run, to make sure the chosen message would fit, especially the message for today. Love. Honour. Cherish. She didn't want to run cherish off the edge.

Although that might be appropriate, she thought. Of the last seven cakes she made, five were for marriages that lasted less than a year. One of the first ones broke up before the bills were paid. Now, she did cake baking and decorating strictly for cash. No pay, no cake.

She finished the job an hour later, in time to take her creation to the bride's home. The mother of the bride was paying for the cake, and she decided to put the words from the service on top, under the little plastic bride and groom. No one would notice the words. By the time they got to the cake, in her experience of weddings, they were all too drunk even to taste it.

She placed the cake on the floor of the green 1995 Honda, in the space left when Tony took out the back seat. The mother didn't order those little packets of cake the single girls put under their pillows to dream on. Disgusting, she thought: squashed cake as a dreamcatcher.

The address was in the wealthy section of town, on the other side of the river from where Brittany lived. Two tall pillars, like the ones between the layers of her cakes, stood on either side of an iron gate in the ten-foot-high fence. One of the pillars held a button and an intercom. She punched as instructed and the voice told her to come up and around to the back of the house. It was always the back. Her old Honda wasn't fit to be seen, or she wasn't, at the front.

The underling—that's what she called the person sent out of the house to get the cake—the underling. In this neighbourhood, he usually was snootier than the owners of the house. Not this one though. Winston asked her if he could help her, carried in the cake as though it were made of crystal.

"Would you like a cup of tea while I get the money for you?" he asked.

"No, thanks. I'm in a hurry."

"I'll be a moment."

After the moment stretched into twenty minutes, Brittany opened the door a crack. When there was no response, she pushed it further and slipped through and found herself in a corridor. Another door barred her way. Too bad. She walked through into a dining room with a table set for twelve but no people. An archway defined a living room beyond.

She was going to be in trouble for this one, she thought but remembered the three hundred dollars they owed her and pressed on. The next obstacle was a pair of French doors, closed. The drapes must have been pulled in the room because the only light she could see through the doors glowed from a lamp on the other side of the room.

Someone shouted, "You...you scoundrel. I lament the day I ever laid eyes on you. Take that, you rat, and that and that."

Shots punctuated the shouting.

Brittany had her hand on the doorknob when she stopped. What business was it of hers if they were killing each other in this vast empty house? She would be in the kitchen, waiting. She scurried back across the rooms and through the door to the kitchen wing. Her legs failed her, and she grabbed the table for support and then sank into a chair. What should she do? Should she call the police? She was searching her purse for her cell when Winston walked back into the room.

"I'm sorry to have been so long," he said. "I had to clear up a bit of mess."

Mess, he called it. A dead body. She didn't hear anything, she reminded herself. She needed her money, and she would go.

Winston handed the cash to her. She forced herself to count the bills twice before tucking them in her pocket. Her hands were shaking, and she could see Winston staring at them.

"Is anything the matter?" he asked.

"No, no nothing. I need to go now. Good-bye," Brittany gabbled as she backed away from him and then ran out the door to her car. Why does he look so puzzled, she thought as she backed the car away from him? He's the one with a dead body to clear up.

Brittany read three papers, watched the news on four different stations and listened to the updates on the radio every hour. By the end of the week, not one word appeared about a murder in the mansion on Moonlight Crescent. How did they hush it up? Someone was dead in that house.

She took to driving by to check it out. Maybe the house was empty now, and they all moved away.

By the end of another week, police stopped her with questions about lurking around the estates. When she told them what she heard, they said they would check.

~

At the end of a month, she saw a notice that the marriage had been annulled. The groom left departed for Europe on the wedding day and hadn't been heard from since.

~

Two months later the house was for sale. Brittany went out of the cake decorating business.

~

The next summer, she went to the movies with Tony. A murder mystery, he said. The movie had been shot in their town, the poster bragged. The house seemed familiar to Brittany. And then she heard those words again, "take that... and that... and that." A movie, she thought. They were rehearsing a movie.

THE BIRTHDAY PRESENT

Wishes shouldn't always come true. The Birthday Present appeared in Ducts.org, issue 24, December, 2009.

19

THE BIRTHDAY PRESENT

*S*omewhere a mourning dove was singing its early morning wake-up. Paul stirred and glanced at the clock. Five in the morning. The sun was slanting through his bedroom window, and in a minute or two it would bounce from the mirror straight into his eyes. His feet hit the floor with a thud as he remembered this was the day he was going fishing with his grandfather. Today was his tenth birthday.

Grandpa was spooning loose green tea from the box - he called it a caddy - he kept on the sideboard. The old pot on the stove was steaming, ready for the leaves. Paul sat down in front of the bread and jam and waited for him to pour the tea into the china mugs, his with a golden retriever printed on it and Grandpa's with a boxer.

"Are we going to take the carriage today?"

The ancient vehicle lived in the barn along with the old horse called Penny who knew the way to the fishing hole as he did. Grandpa only took them out on fine days.

"I think it might rain this morning. Too wet for the old girl."

Paul didn't know whether he meant the carriage or the horse, but if they didn't take them, they would drive in the model A Ford.

"Do you want me to dig some worms?" Paul asked, his words muffled by his last bite of bread.

"No, I put a minnow trap in the beaver pond last night. We'll go pick them up before we go to the fishing hole."

Grandpa took his dishes and Paul's to the sink and stacked them. Grandma would wash them when she got up.

Grandpa' s dad had used the Model A pickup truck to deliver his vegetables and honey to market during the thirties. He had bought it new before everyone lost all their money in the thirties. Paul wondered how all the money was lost and where it went to. He wondered if someone had stolen and hidden it, but Grandpa said that wasn't what happened.

He put the fishing gear behind the seat and climbed in beside Grandpa and waited. It always took a little time for the truck to decide to go. After Grandpa pulled on the little knob and pumped a pedal on the floor, the engine caught, and he backed out of the barn.

They drove down the lane towards the back of the farm, turned into the track that led to the pond, and stopped at the edge of the bush. The ground was too wet to take it any further. They walked across the beaver meadow, with all the little ends of trees the beavers had felled sticking up through the grass.

"Where's the trap?"

"At the other end of the pond."

Frogs jumped out of the way, and a sleepy turtle ambled across their path as they made their way along the pond. The sunshine disappeared behind heavy gray clouds, pushed across the sky by a wind that was making little waves on the pond. Paul hoped it wouldn't rain too hard because the fishing was only good in a light rain.

Grandpa pulled at a line that snaked through the grass and into the pond, but the line was cut and the trap gone.

"Why would someone take our minnows, Grandpa?"

"To go fishing," he answered.

He wasn't paying much attention to Paul's question. He was squatting on the ground, looking at footprints in the mud at the edge of the water.

"Smooth soles," he said.

Paul knew he wasn't talking to him anymore. He always told Paul he was 'thinking out loud'.

Grandpa's boots left a rough pattern in the mud, and so did his rubber boots. Why would anyone go fishing in Sunday shoes? But he didn't ask Grandpa because he was following the footprints up the hill.

Paul struggled to keep up with him as they crossed through the sugar bush at the top of the hill and started down the other side. The river flowed across the farm at the bottom of the hill. A wide spot in the river, under an overhanging willow tree, formed Paul's fishing hole.

Grandpa stopped where they could see the river bank. Two men sat by a tiny fire while a third man tossed a line into the water. He didn't have a real pole, just a stick with a line on it. The missing minnow trap sat on the back beside him. When his line was in the water, he eased the trap back into the river.

Grandpa moved back into the bush a little and stared at the men by the river. Paul heard a strange little sound, a click, but Grandpa didn't seem to notice until a man came out of the trees behind him.

"Whatcha lookin' at, old man?" he growled.

A gun was in the man's hand, his finger on the trigger.

"You better come down to the river."

He waved the gun at Grandpa who pulled Paul to him but didn't say a word. They walked down the hill single file with Paul first, then Grandpa, then the man with the gun.

The other three men stood up as they walked into the makeshift camp.

"What the hell?" said one.

"Who's this?" said another.

The third man stared. Paul stood behind Grandpa and held tight to his arm. Grandpa's muscles grew hard inside the sleeve of his green work shirt.

"It's been a long time, Mike," Grandpa said.

Paul thought he sounded sad and mad, the way he did when the calf died because the vet took too long in coming.

"Why did you bring them down here?" Mike asked the man with the gun.

"They was watching."

The man sounded scared of Mike, Paul thought, like he was the one with the gun.

"We gotta get out of here," one of the other men said.

"What we goin' to do with these two?" the man with the gun asked Mike.

"Nothing. Let's go."

"But they seen us."

"So what? They won't say anything."

"How do you know? This guy knows you. He'll tell the cops."

Grandpa's arm shook a little.

"Mike, this is Paul," was all Grandpa said. He was staring at Mike as though he wanted to memorize him.

"He looks good," was all Mike said.

Mike turned to the others. "We have to get out of here. Go. I'll be right behind you. I'll take care of this."

He pulled a gun from his pocket as the others started out the trail. He stared after them until they disappeared around a curve. Grandpa put his arm around Paul's shoulders and pulled him behind him.

Mike fired two shots into the water. "You'd better go. One of those guys might decide to help me bury the bodies."

Grandpa didn't say a word, but turned to walk back up the hill. Half-way up Paul looked back. Mike was watching them as they climbed.

Grandpa didn't say anything all the way back to the farmhouse, and even after he sat down at the kitchen table. Grandma gave them both cups of tea and held Grandpa's hand when he started to cry. Paul didn't want to watch Grandpa cry, and went into the front room, to sit on the piano stool and wait for Grandma to come.

Most of the pictures were pictures of him when he was a baby and at school. One of them was a wedding picture. Grandpa and Grandma stood beside the bride. She was looking up and smiling at the man beside her, holding his hand. His parents, Grandpa said, but he had never seen them. Grandpa told him his mother had died and his father gone away.

Paul had imagined his father a hero, working on top-secret government jobs, or as a spy, trying to understand why he never came back. He peered at the man in the picture. He was young, like the teenagers who worked on the farm in the summer, and he looked like Mike.

Paul walked back into the kitchen.

"Was that my dad, back there in the bush?"

"Yes."

It was his birthday, and he met his father. Paul sat in front of the old piano and cried.

FIRE OF LOVE

Eavesdropping can be dangerous. Fire of Love was published in Confabulation 4 by Wynterblue Publishing, North Bay, Ontario in 2010.

20

FIRE OF LOVE

*T*he heavy oak doors of the mansion in Forest Hill opened only for those considered worthy because of birth. The Ladies' Recreation Club, founded more than a hundred years before, provided a sanctuary from the hurly-burly of daily life, a place of quiet contemplation, lovely gardens, improving lectures and delicious food.

The founders established strict rules. Only the direct descendants on the female side could belong. That is they were strict before Amanda Harris-Lutyens, and her coterie hijacked the board and forced through an amendment allowing stepdaughters to join. Amanda's group thought only the elderly would object. However, the elderly enjoyed their busy lives too much to worry about it. They lunched, and drank white wine, and gossiped and watched the bare-chested gardeners at work on the estate.

No, it was member Robin Hardcastle, fifty years old, saddled for life with a name from the nursery, frustrated by her lack of power at work and at home, who had been so adamantly against the change. Now she sat in the parlour, rigid on a straight-backed Victorian chair, and went over the details of the meeting. She remembered Lance Townsend, the manager, taking the copious notes he transcribed, printed, and distributed by eight o'clock the next morning. And by eleven o'clock, Alice Tomkins-Stout arrived with her third husband's daughter for lunch. And who had her mother been? Alice declined to say.

Robin's chair gave her a full view of the lawn, but not of the parlour. A Japanese screen shielded her from the other occupants, of whom, at this moment, there were none. She noted the number of breaks the new man took and reminded herself to complain to Lance about him.

The door to the parlour opened with a faint screech, and then footsteps walked over toward her end of the room. Someone sat down at the telephone stand and dialled. Moments later, she recognizedLance's voice.

"Hi. How ya doin? I got your message, but I waited until I had a little private time. Are you coming over soon?"

Robin's back stiffened. How familiar he sounded. Surely he wasn't speaking to a member? Her hearing was going a little, and she strained to hear the conversation. What did he say about love? He repeated it.

"Fire of Love. I can't wait to show you. Guarantee you'll love it."

Robin sat for a long moment until Lance had left the room. She went to the desk and pushed the redial button on the phone.

"Kilgour residence."

"I'm sorry, I have the wrong number," she said and hung up.

So Amy Kilgour, the stepdaughter of Amanda's best friend and co-conspirator, Jane Simpson, was coming to enjoy Lance's love fire. How could she be so common? This was the very reason Robin had objected to the rule change. Undue influence, that's what it was. Her granddaughter was a member and she was only twelve. If this continued, who knew what would happen? Her thoughts went on and on. Soon she convinced herself that Lance was a potential pedophile and she must stop him. She hurried to her car and drove home.

Lance looked up from his desk in the front office. He wrote his blog on his lunch hour and had added the news that his book of poetry, titled Songs from My Garden was going to be published. His twin passions, poetry and gardening and only one made him any money. Amy walked in the front door, holding her head high as her step-mother instructed.

"Look like you belong and you will," she said to her that morning.

"Amy, hi. Come on out to the garden, and I'll show you," said Lance.

Robin's Mercedes stopped at the portico. She rushed out and up the stairs, pushing open the heavy doors. The foyer was empty.

She ran out the French doors towards the more secluded areas of the garden. She knew where he would take the girl. The "giardino Segreto", the secret garden he built behind the tall hedges.

As she approached, she heard Amy's delighted laughter and the deeper rumble of Lance's voice. Shameless, shameless. She pulled the small automatic from her pocket. At first, she couldn't see them through eyes misty with tears of rage, but then there they were. Amy knelt on the ground, looking up at Lance.

Robin stumbled towards them, intent on saving Amy, when the girl said, "They're so lovely, Lance. I must have some for myself."

Have some for herself? What was the poor deluded child talking about? They turned towards her as she shouted at them to stop. Lance pulled Amy up and shielded her behind him.

"Stop what Mrs Hardcastle? What are you doing with that gun?"

"I heard what you said to her, telling her to come and see your fire of love. You have to be stopped before your sick behaviour spreads like an infection to all the young girls."

Her hand shook as she aimed at his body mass as her husband had taught her.

Amy stepped away from Lance pointing to the bed behind her

filled with the fiery red blossoms and white and green striped leaves of the flower.

She screamed at Robin, "Fire of Love" is a tulip. He's showing me a tulip, a tulip, for god's sake. Are you crazy?"

"A tulip. He's showing you a tulip?"

Robin's shaking fingers dropped the gun and covered her face.

"He's showing me a tulip. Lance likes flowers and other men, not girls. That's why the board hired him. Didn't you know."

Lance and Amy backed away from her and then ran to the house. Lance said, "I'll call 911."

He was calling the police, she thought. They would arrest her. She would go to prison. She picked up the gun and walked over to the bed of tulips. She bent down and picked a flower, and raised the gun to her head. They found her face down on the bed, surrounded by the tulips.

After the police and the coroner and the crime investigators and the reporters had come and gone, Lance sat down to add to his blog.

According to Persian legend, the first tulips sprang up from the drops of blood shed by a lover, and for a long time, the tulip was the symbol of avowed love.

Poor Robin, what flowers would grow from her blood, spilled, not for love but for hate and fear.

THE DECISION

A single decision taken and life changes forever. This story won first prize in the Sentinel Literary Quarterly, London, U.K. December, 2012

21

THE DECISION

*G*eorgina walked out of the consultant's office. At least she supposed she was walking, or maybe she was floating, just above the floor. No, she could hear her footsteps as she reached the hallway. The carpet didn't extend out here.

The floor was a sort of acrylic resin, mimicking marble, or so the architect must have thought. But it was only acrylic. A monomerous structure, no, polymerous, she remembered. Formed the way humans are formed. First the single cell, monomerous, and then the exciting union with the winner of the race, his tail slashing as he swam upstream to his prize. The single cell remained single but doubled its payload. Now, the dance of the deoxyribonucleic acid strands as they twisted into the classic form, the division, and then there were two cells, then four. She could calculate the divisions needed to reach the gastrula, the embryo she carried, secure within her abdominal muscles, her bony pelvis, the thick-walled uterus. The cells had begun to differentiate, to form the germ layers from which all the organs would emerge.

She had studied it since she was eighteen, first for her BSc, then her Masters, on the reproductive life of the paddle-tail newt, and finally her PhD, which correlated amphibian and human reproduction. She had chosen not to experience it herself. She had no time for the care of a vulnerable infant of any species, especially her own. But that was before last week, a mere ten days ago, and before last year when he came to work in her department.

Georgina heard the consultant's voice. "It's very early, of course. You can take a little time to decide what's best for you."

She stood at the elevator, watched her face in the mirror at the end of the hall. She hadn't changed. She supposed she would if she were to let this go on. Her features would soften, and the sharp edges of her cheekbones would disappear. She patted her flat abdomen that took six hours a week at the gym to maintain and imagined it billowing away from her.

Two men exited the elevator and stared at her as she knew they would, as men always had. It was so easy to be the femme fatale of the Science Department, Biology division, taking hearts as easily as she took tricks at bridge, until he came, last year.

He prowled the department and invaded her dreams, appearing as a predatory black cat, a Jaguar, or sometimes a white wolf with burning eyes. He seemed immune to her, and she tried to avoid his hallway, his door where the even the tall letters of his name seduced her.

One night, many months ago, she found him standing at her car when she came out to leave for the night. A drink turned into dinner turned into a weekend, and then they were living together. Her work didn't suffer. She seemed to be more creative in her hypotheses, more secure in her conclusions.

She found herself watching the children in the daycare on the first floor. Each tiny human would run to its mother at the end of the day, putting arms up to be lifted, embraced, assured that the world was safe. She felt a strange ache, almost a hunger when she looked at them.

They agreed not to have children. Both their careers involved long nights, unpredictable hours, trips abroad; it was the wisest course.

The medical arts building stood across from the park in the middle of campus. The path to the other side, and her office took her along the pond and across a tiny bridge, in a miniature Japanese landscape. She stood on the bridge, watching the flicker of the silver and gold koi, remembering what he had said when she told him.

"What are you going to do about it?" You, not we. In an instant, their life changed. He had insisted on no birth control, for him at any rate, and she couldn't take the pills. The little copper coil or whatever it was had failed, and now she had to do something about it.

Georgina walked on, past the desert garden, looking at plants that bloomed in the inhospitable sand and stone. He didn't look at her anymore; didn't run his eyes over her body in the mornings when she emerged naked from the shower or stood on the secluded terrace with her face turned to the rising sun. It had only been three days, but now she lived with a stranger.

"Why did you do the test?" the doctor had asked her. Why? She knew somehow; she felt a change, a shift in the core of her self.

She left the park and strolled down the boulevard to the stone building that held the offices and labs of the biology division. Soon that would change. They were moving, exchanging the art deco lines and embellishments for a modern high-rise closer to the other divisions of the department. It was all for the best, she supposed. New labs, more lecture space, air-conditioning that worked, and a daycare for all the children meant the department could attract more and younger people. Her child would run to meet her at the end of a long afternoon, bringing her the treasures from a day of finger-painting and cut-and-paste.

She shared her office with another new professor, David. He had left a note on her desk. Max called. Make a decision, he had said. She stared out the window at the campus.

The doctor said she had time. But the time had come and gone. She thought about the gastrula, serene in its little cocoon. She thought she would call her Grace.

187

COMING HOME

Reconciliation and a journey home. Coming Home appeared in the Camroc Press, September, 2009

<<<<>>>>

22

COMING HOME

The elevator door opened to the familiar sounds of trays being put back on the dietary carts, nurses calling loudly to elderly patients, families murmuring as they stood in tight formation outside a door, waiting for the doctor's visit to be over, and under it all the faint sounds of people in pain. I heard them all my working life, always in the background to my daily rounds.

I wasn't working today but coming to visit an old friend who was recovering from a fall on the ice and a broken femur.

One of the voices querulous, musical and loud seemed familiar. Familiar and unsettling. I looked in an open door, and there she was, Aunt Tillie, my mother's oldest friend, and terror of my childhood. I hadn't seen her for the ten years since my mother died.

Somehow she knew I was there, and turned that awful glare towards me.

"Althea, is that you? Get in here," she ordered, and like always, I obeyed. I kissed her translucent skin when she pointed to an acceptable spot on her cheek.

"I didn't know you were sick," I said.

Her hand, warm and strong in my memory, felt cold.

"Dying, dear, or will be soon, if I don't let them cut me open and remove most of my insides."

I struggled to keep tears from flowing. She had always been there: reinforcing my mother's rules as she raised the three of us without a father; holding my hand when I had my appendix out and my brother broke his arm all on the same day, and our mother couldn't be with both of us; standing proudly with my mother the day I graduated from medical school.

"What is it?"

"Cancer, dear. In the womb. I think it has spread from the way they talk."

"There's treatment that's good for that," I said, relieved. Maybe it had been confined, and she had misunderstood.

"No, Althea."

She squeezed my hand.

"Look at it straight."

The old admonition, whenever I had broken the rules or wanted to imagine a more hopeful outcome than was realistic.

"Dr. Lang said they couldn't cure it, but can help me live a while longer. I said no. I'm going home today. They are arranging home care."

Home care. The last thing that I imagined her agreeing to. Strangers cleaning her house and her body.

"Are you okay with that?"

"No, but staying here is worse."

Suddenly tired, she closed her eyes and seemed to drift a little, into sleep or at least out of immediate awareness. She nursed my mother during her last illness when I had been in London, working on my fellowship. I couldn't be there for my mother or her. There had been no words of reproach, but I thought I could see it every time Tillie looked at me at the funeral. I grew a hard knot of anger and resentment in my soul then and carried it still.

She had been my mother's constant companion after my father left us. I owed her for loving my mother and caring for her all those years. My guilt had kept me away. Now as I looked at her tired, familiar face, I knew that I had been hurt and angry at the change in their relationship from friends to life partners. A change I wasn't able to acknowledge or accept until now.

She opened her eyes again.

"Do you want to come home with me?"

"It won't be easy, Althea. You know how we clash."

I heard the words but saw the hope and relief in her eyes.

"Nobody promised easy."

I could hear her voice in my head as I said her own old words to her. She smiled, and patted my hand and drifted off to sleep.

Two days later, I took Tillie home, settled her into a chair on the front porch where she could watch the world and made us tea.

She rocked gently in the warm summer air, lightness entered my heart, and I, too, had come home.

ALSO BY VIRGINIA WINTERS

Murderous Roots

The Facepainter Murders

No Motive for Murder

The Child on the Terrace

The Jewelled Egg Murders

Dangerous Journeys Boxed Set

If you have enjoyed my short stories or any of my books, please leave a review on Amazon.com.